BABYSITTER
BLOODBATH ™

A NOVELIZATION

PUPPET COMBO ®

+

REGINA WATTS

Concept & Original Video Game: Vague Scenario LLC
Text: Regina Watts
Typesetting: M. F. Sullivan
Cover: Patrick Driscoll

Puppet Combo® Online: https://puppetcombo.com
Regina Watts Online: https://hrhdegenetrix.com

PROLOGUE

1960

SOME HOUSES were haunted: the Burr house was traumatized.

Who could blame it? The family had lived a good life in its walls. So far as anyone could tell, they were happy there. "So far as anyone could tell" was happy enough.

Happiness aside, Pamela Burr loved that house. Maybe that was why, after her death, the building's molecules seemed altered. When she stepped into its living room for the first time, she said to her husband, Neoklaus, "This is where I want to raise a family."

And that was what they did. First, they had a daughter. Then, they had a son—a baby still cooing in its cradle on the fatal night that Pamela, stuck before the stove, overlooked a roiling cauldron of pasta water.

"Ginny," said Pamela to the empty room, "go ahead and set the table, would you?"

"But I'm busy," protested hallway wall outside the kitchen.

"I'm sure it can wait, whatever it is. I wish you wouldn't fool around in there so much... Could hurt yourself on a nail."

Pamela banged her pronged spoon against the edge of the pot to shake it free of water. A few burning drops splashed off and stung her skin. She barely noticed.

She looked at the clock. Neoklaus would be home any minute.

"Come on, sweetie," Pamela urged her daughter, provoking a sigh from the crawlspace whose tiny entrance lay beneath the stairs to the second floor.

The space itself was narrow. How Ginny could stand it in there, Pamela could never understand. Like a coffin, that tight hollow in the wall.

Pamela had intended to use it as a storage space, but the area was so cramped that she worried about getting things out again. Over time, Ginny claimed this empty space as a playroom for herself, and her mother didn't really mind because it made her easy to find.

The girl, still behind the clown mask she'd worn

since a party a few weeks prior, wiggled through the small door while dusting off her overalls. Only as she entered the kitchen did she push the plastic mask atop her head to see her mother's work.

Pamela smiled down at her daughter. "Just what are you doing in there, anyway?"

"Visiting Aslan," answered the witty child.

Ah, yes! Ginny had been taken with those funny Lewis books since her grandmother bought her the first few. Pamela had read them all to her. They'd been wonderful! A wild, adventuresome story.

Too bad Neoklaus had never heard any of it—he was always elsewhere in the house, doing something by himself. Pamela was never sure what.

"Well, just get the table set and you can go back."

After dragging her three-legged stool to the cabinet, the girl spent a bit of time going back and forth across to do as her mother asked.

Soon enough she was back in Narnia.

Alone with her thoughts, Pamela looked at the clock again. Yes—yes, any minute, Neoklaus would be home.

He certainly was late, though, wasn't he? Maybe that was what made her so nervous that night.

There wasn't any other reason she could find: no reason at all for her to be so on-edge when her husband finally opened the living room door.

"There you are!" Joy lit her voice at his footfall. "Did you have a good day at the factory? I'm just exhausted, myself—little Tommy had an awful time going down for his nap, you'd never believe it."

Neoklaus's heavy steps terminated at the threshold of the kitchen. Pamela looked over her shoulder to smile at him. Then, brooding again over her pasta, she plucked up her spoon with one hand and the strainer with the other.

Her husband's steps continued into the kitchen. She asked without looking, "Why don't you take off your boots before you sit down, Neoklaus? Looks like it's almost time to get you a new pair! Those old ones are so—"

Her eyes widened at a sharp explosion of fiery pain in her right shoulder blade. Another, now in her left shoulder. What was happening? What was happening? The strainer and spoon both tumbled from her hands.

"Neoklaus—" Wild-eyed, she stumbled back against the pot of boiling water. Fresh from the butcher block, the knife gleamed with Pamela's blood in her own husband's hand. "Neoklaus—"

There was no making sense of it. No understanding, though her brain did try. It was natural to try to understand was happening when your own husband came home before dinner, took up one of your kitchen knives, and stabbed you to death with it.

He stared into her eyes while the blade sank again and again into her flesh. Its recently sharpened metal opened her skin so easily that some of the penetrations didn't even hurt—but more of them did. Some were so sharp that it was like her whole body had caught fire.

Somewhere their daughter was screaming. Pamela realized vaguely that she had, in an attempt to gain purchase, stuck her hand against the pot of boiling water while the other lifted to futilely against the blows.

She didn't feel the hot metal pot, but she felt that knife. Each time a new wound opened up to pour blood down her hand, her wrist, her forearm, she felt it with a kind of hyper-clarity. As if the pain were the only thing that existed.

"Neoklaus—"

Her legs gave out from under her amid the suffusion of pain, the severity of her blood loss.

"Neoklaus— I don't understand—"

Pamela's quivering body slid upon the tile floor and came to rest in the fast-developing pool of its own blood.

With her last scraps of consciousness, Pamela remembered their daughter. Oh! Her body was so weak: but, somehow, she lurched forward as Neoklaus stepped away—lurched forward and grabbed his dirty boot, begging, "Please—Neoklaus, please don't—"

He kicked her in the head so hard it felt like her brain came loose inside her skull.

While she sobbed, still searching for some explanation for why this was happening to her—for why this, of all ways, was the way she was going to die—Neoklaus bent over to catch her hair in his fist.

With a quick, cold slash of the knife, Neoklaus cut Pamela's throat. A crimson wave splattered out of her neck and down the front of her dress; over her dream house's carefully clean floor; across her husband's filthy black boots.

Some of the stabs may have been so precise she hadn't felt them, but she did feel the slitting of her throat. In a single stroke the blade cleanly severed the molecules of flesh, tendons, veins. The feeling of having her tissues split by her husband was written on Pamela's face as she died, mute, in a pool of her own blood.

Neoklaus left boot prints on his way back to the living room. The urgent whisper of his daughter's high voice carried through the house as tough its walls were made of paper.

So did Neoklaus's footsteps. On his coming, the wide-eyed girl gasped into the phone's black receiver, "Please, operator, please hurry—oh—"

Leaving the wall-mounted device hanging from its cord, Ginny scrambled for the security of her crawlspace. The girl was red-faced and sobbing, her words unintelligible amid her tears. "Daddy! Why would you do this—why would you hurt Mommy like this?"

He didn't answer. The girl didn't wait for one. She tried to shut the door of the crawlspace after her, but quickly found that she shouldn't have delayed for that, either.

The door slammed off its hinges as Burr reached in after his daughter. One great hand grabbed around in the dark, grasping exposed wood and open air before finally catching one kicking leg.

"No," screamed Ginny, "no, please! I love you! Please!"

Immeasurably weaker than a full-grown man, all Ginny could do to try and save her own life was grab hold of whatever she could. An exposed beam helped her for a few seconds. At the next hard jerk of her leg and the horrific thought that the limb might be pulled from its socket, she lowered her weeping head against the beam. In a last-ditch effort, Ginny tried to pray.

As she realized she was too afraid to remember the words to even the most basic prayer, her father jerked her leg again and she cried out.

Her hair was torn by a crooked nail exposed from the same beam. The house itself was what tore the mask from her hair when, with a final wrench, Neoklaus pulled his daughter out of the crawlspace.

He wasted no time.

Ginny screamed more than Pamela had. Pamela had just been confused: Ginny was afraid, betrayed, keenly aware of what was about to happen to her.

The girl threw her small hands over her head as though to block out the vision of her fate. In so doing, she exposed her torso to Burr's knife.

The tearing of denim, as the knife plunged into her entrails, seemed almost as loud as her shrieks—almost as loud as the crying of the baby awoken upstairs.

By the time Burr was finished killing his daughter, her blue overalls had turned a purple-red so dark that it had more in common with black.

Blood coated the white palms limp on either side of her body, but no matter the blood she lost, no matter how dead she was, her eyes still seemed to stare. This corpse gazed in shock at the face of its father and killer. Neoklaus looked only at the glistening knife still ready in his hand.

The baby's wailing filled the house, but it wasn't loud enough to drown out the police cruisers parking outside. His movements at once more urgent than they'd been seconds before, Burr threw the knife into the far back of the crawlspace.

He did not even stoop to see that it came to rest tucked behind a beam. All that mattered was getting it out of his hand. Throwing it away like the family it had destroyed: that was what was important. This done, he shut the door and followed the sound of the crying upstairs.

There he was, in his cradle. Doing harm to nobody. Only screaming like he understood what was about to happen to him. Through the window of the nursery, voices shouted from the street. "Open up, Burr! Nobody has to get hurt—just come out! Let's figure out what's happened."

When no response was forthcoming, somebody cursed. The banging of the front door began at the same second Burr picked up the sobbing infant. As if knowing what occurred within the house, the banging grew more urgent.

Burr's lips peeled back from his teeth. At first, when Burr's jaws pierced the cloth of the white onesie as easily as the blade had eviscerated Pamela, Tommy's sobs increased. The pressure of Burr's teeth intensified as blood surged into his mouth. Downstairs, the slam of the front door was impressive competition for the sound of the child's last scream.

When Burr tore his teeth away, having liberated a mouthful of the baby's tender guts, the grip of his hand tightened. Something ripped.

Fabric? No.

He didn't even realize he'd torn the child's head off. Not until he looked back down to find one half in each hand.

The nursery door burst open. Police surged in, guns drawn.

"Hands up, you sick son-of-a-bitch! Oh, my God— put up your hands, put up your fucking hands!"

He obeyed once he had thrown the headless corpse of his infant against the wall and its soft body burst like an overripe melon.

1.

1982

MONROE STATE HOSPITAL had seen more than its share of violent inmates. Among the depraved minds consigned to its many rooms, Neoklaus Burr was just another face. Everybody there had an awful story. Nurse Trixie wasn't impressed by any of them.

"I'll kill you," an inmate might scream at her.

"I know," she'd say, "I know you will. Just take your medication, now—thank you! Was that so hard?"

"Your mother sucked my dick in Vietnam," another would holler while the orderlies ducked a hurled lunch tray.

"Mr. Thornburg, if you please! We wouldn't have

to restrain you like this if you didn't throw things at us…"

Another: "The voices! The voices—I wish they'd stop talking, just for even a second—"

Her cool response: "Well, why don't we see if a little art therapy helps us today?"

Yes, Nurse Trixie was unflappable. It was her compassion that did it. Maybe it was thanks to the novel by that Kesey fellow, but most people seemed to imagine sanitarium nurses as cruel tyrants ruling their patients' lives with iron fists.

But Trixie understood what these folks went through. She understood they were suffering. She understood that, long before the hospital ever put them under lock and key, they had been trapped in the prisons of their own mental illnesses.

She pitied them, these patients. She pitied them, and by holding on to that pity she didn't permit herself any room for fear. What was there to be afraid of, after all? These were sick people. Truly ill.

Most of them wouldn't have done the least harm to anyone under any circumstances; and those that already had, well, they couldn't do it again. They were treated fairly. They were treated as people and, especially after the sanitarium's recent change in management, they were shown actual compassion.

Trixie loved that. She loved being allowed to take care of these people as if they were actually ill and in need of care. She loved seeing the difference kind treatment made in so many of their lives. She loved feeling confident and composed before even the most disordered patients, as though she might be a model for the responsible people they could be if and when they recovered.

But—

Despite all her confidence, despite her charisma and compassion, she had to admit that one patient was very unnerving to her.

Neoklaus Burr never said a word.

Everybody had tried to get him to speak. Before Trixie's arrival, therapists had sat on the other side of a table from the man for cumulative hours. All the while he stared as if willing the person at whom he looked to die on the spot.

Everyone who worked at the hospital agreed that Burr was the most disturbing of all their disturbed patients. This wasn't just because of his silence, though.

Once, when new at the sanitarium, Trixie had gotten curious about this silent man always confined to his cell. When the sanitarium changed hands amid its period of reform, most of the patients began to enjoy things like scheduled leisure time and therapeutic activities. Painting. Bird-watching.

So far as Trixie could tell, Burr was never permitted anything. In fact, she wasn't sure that she'd seen him liberated from his solitary confinement for so much as a therapist's session. Wondering why, she looked up his file.

How she regretted it! Oh, it was awful. Nurses tended to exchange patients' stories by word-of-mouth, but nobody really discussed Burr. After reading up on him, Trixie understood why.

No crime scene photos were included in the file, but she could imagine it all vividly nonetheless. From then on, every time she happened to glance Burr's hard face through the window of his cell door, she couldn't help her shudder.

The face of a man who stabbed his daughter to death; the face of a man who had eaten his infant after killing his wife.

Nobody liked to look into that face. Consequently, most people avoided any duty that forced them to interact with Burr.

But somebody had to do it.

It might as well have been brave, compassionate Trixie, who could find empathy in her heart for anyone in the world. Any ailing soul. No matter how dark that soul seemed.

So, Trixie gave Burr her best smile every night she saw him. She had a lot of other patients, understand, which made it tough to find time to get to Burr. And when she did get to him, it was always in-and-out. You could even have accused her of rushing.

One time, she dropped his pills before giving him his medication. That was very embarrassing. Trixie had never done a thing like that before. She had to ask herself what the problem was.

Why was she frightened of him? Of course, he'd done horrible things...but so had a lot of the other inmates.

There was a very soft-spoken man not very many rooms down from Burr. Talk about cannibalism! This patient had eaten his own mother's brains after her accidental death in the midst of a domestic dispute.

Yet somehow Trixie wasn't afraid of him at all. The brain-eater was a polite man. He played chess with the other patients.

Strike that. He was *allowed to play chess with the other patients.*

That was Trixie's problem, she realized at last.

It was the hospital's perception of Burr that was getting to her. Her colleagues, her supervisors—everyone had made him out to be some kind of horrific monster. Some enormous demon. A man somehow so much worse than all the other ill people in the hospital.

Why was that? Because of the deaths of the children, she supposed. The baby.

And while yes, of course, it was incomprehensible... as more privileges were introduced to the higher-functioning patients, and even lower-functioning ones earned more second chances, Nurse Trixie's poor, tender heart just broke to see even this man—even this worst among the worst of them—abandoned in his cell.

She resolved to be better. It only took one person to make a difference in someone else's life, after all. That was why Trixie had become a nurse. She wanted to make a difference: to be there for the downtrodden, like a kind of angel. The other patients responded so well to being treated like people. Surely Burr was no exception to the rule.

Best to start slow.

First, Trixie shook off the guard who accompanied her while she delivered medication to the more challenging patients. "I'm glad to have you with me," she told him with a friendly pat on the forearm. "It's just this outfit of yours! The tie puts our patients on-edge."

"All right, Trixie…you'll radio for me if you run into trouble, though, won't you?"

Oh, trouble! Trouble, nothing. Even the worst patients were no trouble to her. Most of them even liked her. The ones that didn't were the sort who didn't like anyone, so it wasn't anything special when something foul came out of their mouths in exchange for their daily dose of lithium. Trixie wouldn't have any trouble. She was confident of that.

Just like she was confident that tonight, this crisp October night, would be the first night of Neoklaus Burr's better life.

"Mr. Burr?"

In the high-security ward, patient's rooms resembled prison cells. This was true even down to the slot in the door, a small rectangular cut-out used for restraints, food, and the passage of medication.

However, many inmates couldn't be trusted to take their medication. In that case, nurses would have to let themselves into the room. Though they were not often restrained anymore, staff interactions with violent patients tended to be supervised by orderlies or guards like the very one whose help Trixie rejected.

When she was hired, most veteran staff members had advised her to pass Burr his medication through the door slot and move on. All had said that talking to him was useless, if not actively dangerous. Trixie, however, knew better than that.

She spoke to Burr through the slot, struggling to see him in his cell. Was he against the wall?

"Mr. Burr," she repeated, "it's time for your medication. But, I was thinking— It's a beautiful evening, and you don't have a window in your cell."

While straightening up, Trixie removed her keyring and jingled through its contents, her other hand poised casually on the cart arrayed with paper cups of pills. "Why don't you come out once you've had your medication? You could watch the sunrise from the observation window. Oh! The way the light twinkles on the duck pond, it's just marvelous."

Beaming ear-to-ear, Trixie pushed her master key into the lock of Burr's door. Her own soul rattled with satisfaction as the tumbler clicked. "Just when was the last time you saw a duck, Mr. Burr?"

No response. Well, she'd get him talking soon enough! Pleased as she could be, Trixie pushed open the door to the cell, and Neoklaus stepped out to grip the small woman by the head. As soon as he had confident hold of her, he smashed her skull against the stones lining the doorway of his cell.

The overwhelming pain was so instant that Trixie had no time to scream. It reminded her of all the times she had ever hit her head on a car roof, or the door of an open cabinet: that feeling of her skull being split.

Only now, it was really being split. Now she could feel, on the second impact, the tearing open of her scalp and the terrific shattering of wet, red bone.

The man's huge hand clenched her face all the tighter. She at last remembered to scream, but the third slam dislocated her jaw and crunched her cheekbone so severely that the sound was more of a wheeze that trailed off into a gurgle.

The keys fell from her hand. Burr's free one caught them before the gained much distance. Blood rushing from her nose and mouth, Trixie slid to the floor and convulsed. Burr stepped neatly over her and looked around the hall.

Inhale, exhale. This was freedom, Neoklaus. The very sanitarium seemed to breathe with him: its stones rose and fell like the barrel of his chest as, one by one, Burr opened cells. One, two, three. Someone at the end of the hall shouted, "Hey, you!"

Burr crammed the keys into the hands of the

man he had just released. The killer then strode in the direction of the security guard. The uniformed man's expression changed, moving from a look of authoritarian expectation to sheer, human terror.

This gig had been a sweet one. Trixie, who lay in a twitching heap in the doorway of Burr's cell, had been lulled into a false sense of security by the culture of the sanitarium.

The guard was the same. He had gotten lax. He carried a gun but hadn't used it for years. He hadn't thought he'd ever use it.

Of course, he never would. Not with that trembling hand—not with the way he fumbled at his holster.

In twelve long strides Burr cleared the distance down the hall. He was to the guard just when the doughy man had the weapon in his hand.

The guard leveled the muzzle with Burr's face in time for the killer to snatch his hand, push the weapon away, and use the heel of his palm to crush his nose up into his skull cavity. The guard didn't even have time to scream.

While shaking the blood from his hand, Burr snatched the gun from the dying man's grip. The guard was put out of his misery while, not far from Burr, the shouts of more guards frightened by gunfire rose the alarm.

Neoklaus Burr looked at the security camera poised in the corner of the ceiling, raised the gun, and spent a round in the lens.

2.

SARAH STRUGGLED to listen to a word Jill said. The mall food court buzzed with activity and, through it all, Sarah tried to narrow her focus down to a single conversation.

Two girls a few tables away had been saying something she'd barely caught. Now she strained past the voice of her friend, hoping to hear them repeat it. Her diligence was rewarded.

"—Jack," said one of the girls again.

A few more unintelligible words.

Then: "—birthday, and—"

Jill snapped a finger in front of Sarah's face. "Hello? Earth to Sarah! Are you even listening to me?"

"Sorry! I just remembered I had one more errand to run before we left."

"Well, you'd better hurry." Jill checked her watch and leaned back in her seat, eyebrows lifting. "The mall's closing soon. Do you want to meet me at the entrance?"

"That'd be perfect." Slinging her purse higher up her shoulder, Sarah did a few swift mental calculations. Every penny counted, but she was set to make enough on tomorrow's babysitting job that there was no harm in spending a few extra bucks. Of course, Billy's parents might stiff her again—they were on their last warning, for sure—but making headway with Jack was a worthy cause.

After dusting off her hands and patting her friend's shoulder, Sarah said, "Catch see you soon," and darted in the direction of the escalators.

Was Jack even still around? She happened to see him earlier, a few minutes after she and Jill arrived. No surprise. In their small town, the options for recreation consisted of hitting the mall, going to parties, or bashing mailboxes from their posts while your drunk driver tries to keep from running off the road.

This was all assuming football season had ended, of course. It hadn't just yet, though October more than crisped the air to give that special autumn buzz. Since Jack was on the football team, he must have skipped practice to come hang out.

Weren't people entitled to things like that on birthdays, though? And, anyway, it gave her ideas for presents. Like, maybe she could buy him a jersey of some kind! Not that she knew anything much about sports.

An album? Well, maybe. Everybody liked music. She didn't know what kind of music he liked specifically, though—she'd rather buy him nothing than buy a gift that made her look stupid.

The mall speaker crackled with an announcement. Something about a curfew? She paused near the entrance of a store, trying to make out the tinny words. Very soon, she gave up and shook her head, annoyed.

Two men were exiting the store mid-conversation. Sarah turned back to the entrance just in time for the one with his head turned to slam into her.

"Sorry," she began, looking up at the person who'd been paying even less attention than her. "Oh! Jack!"

"Uh," said the jock with a patronizing laugh that his friend shared. "Do I know you?"

Don't act lame, just be cool. "I'm Sarah." She tacked on her last name and, seeing that got nothing out of his blank stare, tried something else. "We had math together. Like, two years in a row?"

"Oh," he said, eyebrows lifting, "oh, Sarah! I recognize you. What's up?"

He recognized her! Nice of him to say that. Jack was one of the most popular guys in school—everybody knew him and would have loved to be his friend, even if only for the social prestige.

Sarah wasn't worried about that nearly as much as she was interested in his broad shoulders and hard jaw. Jack was one of those strapping boys who grew up in small-town America and, once upon a time, would have found work on a farm or in some form of menial labor. Instead he was playing football and living the life of suburban luxury.

Now that Sarah thought about it, Jack was sort of spoiled. The kind of person who was hard to shop for. If only she had somebody to help her pick something for him…time to take a risk.

"Not much," Sarah began casually. "Today is, like, the birthday of some hot guy I know, so I'm trying to figure out what present to get him."

Blue eyes widening in shock, the good-natured but ultimately not very bright boy put a hand on his chest. "Weird! It's my birthday today, too!"

"Oh my *gosh,*" said Sarah, feigning surprise pretty effectively if she said so herself, "Happy Birthday! What-ever, how crazy."

"I know! Wow, that's a funny coincidence. What are you going to get him?"

Affecting a pout, Sarah shook her head and said, "I don't know! I realized I barely know anything about him. Like, music? Sports teams? Hello?" Sarah knocked herself on the head and laughed. "Guess he's so cute I didn't even think about it before coming here."

"Bet if he's a guy worth your time," said Jack's friend, "he must like the Steers." This earned a laugh and a high-five from Jack. "Go Steers!"

Making a mental note, Sarah allotted, "Maybe. I

guess I was kind of thinking about an album, though."

"That's tough," Jack said, "music is so personal."

Sarah agreed and then casually said, as if it might help her solve her problem, "Well, who do *you like?*"

"Oh, man... America, for sure." Ugh. Yeah, music sure was personal, wasn't it? Sarah maintained a pleasant smile as he also suggested, "Or Fleetwood Mac. Yeah, everybody likes Fleetwood Mac."

"Do they have any new albums?"

"Ah...well, *Mirage* came out in June—I haven't heard it yet, though, so I don't know how it compares. Does he already like Fleetwood Mac? If not, you might just want to give him *Rumors.*"

"You know, I think he *does* like them, actually. Say," looking toward the entrance of the mall, then shooting her best smile up at the athlete, Sarah asked, "could you help me look through the record shop? Do you have a couple minutes?"

"Sure," said Jack, nodding over at his friend. "You want to get the car? I'll meet you."

Okay. Okay! Don't get too excited. Sarah wondered if this sudden awareness of her pulse in her fingertips was just her imagination, or if it was a real physiological effect. Hard to say! Hard to say anything when Jack, big friendly puppy-dog that he was, walked with her to the record store and said on the way there, "I guess you must be nervous, huh?"

"What do you mean?"

"Oh, what? You didn't hear? Yeah! There was, like,

a big break-out at the loony bin earlier tonight—this killer guy, uh, this big guy...what's his name? Nicholas Burr? Whatever. Anyway, I guess he broke out and killed a *ton* of people. They don't have any idea where he is, so they've established a curfew until he's caught."

Sarah blew a raspberry. "Whatever!"

Jack laughed in surprise. "That doesn't freak you out?"

"I mean...I guess, in an abstract way. But what does it have to do with me? Not like I live near the sanitarium or anything."

"Yeah, but he could be anywhere! He could be waiting outside right now. Boo!" Grinning like a jackass, Jack playfully grabbed Sarah's side and succeeded in making her jump. While he howled with laughter, the girl turned her furiously blushing face away and shrugged her purse higher on her shoulder.

"Whatever, jerk!"

"Anyway, I guess it was a super-gnarly crime scene...all kinds of security guards killed. He even murdered some nurses. My uncle's a cop, he called us all freaked out. 'Make sure Jack stays home until this guy gets caught!'"

The boy laughed and rolled his eyes as they ducked into the record store. Behind the counter, the sales clerk looked like she was on the verge of an aneurysm to see customers so close to closing. Sarah smiled at her, anyway, and went straight to the 'F' section to show her they'd be in and out.

"It's cute your uncle cares about you, though," Sarah said, running her fingers along the shrink-wrapped albums. "I hope my parents don't try to keep me from babysitting tomorrow."

She had said this for herself more than for him, but his ears perked. Laughing again, Jack asked, "Babysitting? On a Saturday?"

"I know, it sucks. But it's just for a little while. I'm saving up for a motorcycle."

"Oh, no way! Bitchin'! What kind of hog you want?"

"I'm thinking about a Honda," she said, flipping through the records and smiling to see the cover of *Mirage*. "Is this it?"

"Sure is—hey, you didn't even need me!" He nudged her while she grinned. "A Honda, huh? Most people think about Harley when they think about motorcycles. Why a Honda?"

"Better engineering," she said, trying not to frown at the price on the sticker. Just a little higher than she'd hoped for. Well...not exactly like she could put it back and turn around now.

The transaction was painful, but quick. Once it was over, the salesperson asked if she would need a bag. Butterflies in her stomach, (ugh!), Sarah said, "No, that's not necessary."

She waited until they had emerged from the record store to hand the present over to Jack.

"Here," Sarah said.

He was nice, but he really did get a stupid look on his face sometimes. At least it was a cute kind of stupid look. He blinked down at the extended album and said, "But I thought that was for, like—"

It was always funny to watch somebody put two and two together. Making four in his head, eyes widening all the more, Jack said, "Oh! Hey, was all that— Were you *hitting on me?*"

"Happy Birthday," repeated Sarah, smiling as he accepted the album with unfeigned pleasure.

"Boy, thanks! Wow, I can't believe—you really had me going there. You're slick!" His face had reddened across his cut cheekbones; his grin widened just a little more. Jack pressed the album to the breast of his letter jacket and said, "And pretty cute, too."

"Thanks," she said. "You're not so bad yourself."

With a glance toward the mall security guard, a uniformed man waiting impatiently for them and the rest of the stragglers to leave, Jack looked back at Sarah and asked, "Do you have a pen?"

She did, in fact. When she dug it out of her purse and passed it over, Jack caught her hand in his. Now her own face warmed—boy, that hand of his sure was big.

Big, but gentle. When he wrote his phone number in her hand he was careful not to press too hard. It was kind of sweet. "Call me sometime...maybe we can listen to Fleetwood Mac together."

Beaming, feeling like an evil genius for as well as

that plan came together, Sarah said, "Yeah, sure, maybe. That'd be cool."

"Cool," he said.

They stood staring at one another for another few seconds. Both smiled.

"The mall is now closed," announced the tinny intercom.

Of course, *that* statement was clear enough...

While they laughed and made their way to the mall entrance, Jack said, "Well, thanks again. Be careful out there, all right?"

"Thanks, you too. See you around, Birthday Boy."

A few seconds later, Sarah slammed shut the white door of Jill's car.

"What took you so long?" Shuddering, Jill turned down the news station she'd been listening to. "I've just been, like, sitting here totally creeping myself *out* while you were dragging your butt inside."

"Sorry—but look at *this.*" Gleeful, Sarah thrust her hand in Jill's face. Her friend's expression contorted through several phases before settling on one of shock.

"Um, hello, is this a phone number?"

"*Jack's* phone number."

"Shut up. Shut *up*, is that who you were walking with just now? I couldn't see from here. Shut up!" Scoffing, Jill slapped her hand away. "You bitch!"

Sarah threw her head back and cackled while her friend put the car into gear.

27

"I hate you," Jill continued, stewing with happy jealousy. "You're *such* a freaking jerk! I can't believe you kept me waiting here, all weirded out, just so you could get the Homecoming King's number."

"Whatever. If you promise to be nicer to me, you can have him when I'm done with him. Hey"—Sarah had settled back in her seat, hand in her lap, and the numbers in her palm made her think of something else—"did you hear about that crazy thing at the sanitarium tonight?"

"Uh! No *doy?* That was what I was just freaking telling you about! I knew you weren't listening to me. I'll be sitting there, telling you about something super, like, *stupid*-important, and you just get this glazed look in your eyes like you're—"

Sarah stopped listening.

3.

SCENIC RIVER Park was home to a jogging path so frequently used that no one thought anything of running before dawn. Even as late as October, when the darkness of the pre-sun hours extended beyond all reason, early risers could expect to encounter one another on the path.

That was why Aaron Parsons didn't think anything of the tall man standing in the distance.

Frankly, he wasn't even sure he had seen a man at all. The flashlight he'd jerry-rigged to his headband in lieu of a proper headlamp had a way of bouncing with each step. Though its illumination hinted at a distant silhouette, by the time its beam sprang back up, the figure was gone.

Aaron had probably been seeing things. That, or it was a deer. Either way, he didn't feel the least bit discomforted as he rounded the bend and approached the patch of trees where the figure had stood.

Of course...what if it was something else?

That break-out at the sanitarium: it had been all over the news the night before. A man, a criminal presumed armed and dangerous, had killed multiple nurses, several security guards, and set fire to the head office of the asylum.

All in the space of an hour. Then he had escaped into the night. Citizens were advised to be on the lookout.

But how paranoid could Aaron be? This was River Park. River Park was miles from the sanitarium.

The town was safe and quiet. Even the homeless community was friendly. In the worst case, this was going to be somebody whose sleep had been disturbed by his jog.

Better be respectful. Better be quiet.

Aaron turned down his light and slowed a little, remonstrating himself for his own skittishness. In fact, he still wasn't even sure that he'd seen anybody at all. He'd just mind his business and speed-walk quietly by.

Three minutes later, Burr had finished beating him to death the very flashlight extricated from his headband.

The loose leaves clinging to their trees trembled in the pre-dawn wind. Amid their branches, a murderer double-checked the gun he had taken from the asylum. One more bullet. Could come in handy.

Burr searched the dead body at his feet while River Park looked on in silent horror. Finding nothing more of value, he turned his attention to the issue of the encroaching daylight. He was going to have to find someplace to spend the treacherous daytime hours.

Good thing the town had expanded so much since he last walked free.

4.

SARAH WAVED after her father while his car cruised off into the night. "Thanks again," she called.

How she looked forward to the day when she could hop on her bike and take herself wherever she needed to go! Alone on the dark street, she assessed the Johnson house and reflexively pressed her purse to her heart.

What was she nervous for? This was just a stupid suburban house. Like all the other stupid suburban houses. Why, it wasn't even her first night sitting for the Johnsons.

The problem was all this talk about the sanitarium incident, she guessed. It was all anybody had wanted to discuss that Saturday, and the subject had left her extremely on-edge.

But, of course, it was all stupid. What were the odds

that she—or anybody related to her, for that matter— would encounter this wacko? For all she knew, he'd been captured already. She wasn't sure. She'd spent her day listening to the radio's rock station, hoping they'd play Fleetwood Mac so she could think about Jack.

There was her bravery! Forcing her most pleasant smile to fit upon her face, Sarah made her way up the path to the porch and knocked on the front door.

Mark Johnson opened it a few seconds later, barely bothering to hide the fact that he and his wife must have been waiting for her with bated breath.

"Sarah," said Mark brightly, smoothing his tie while he held the door wide for her, "I'm so glad you could make it! Come on in, let me take your coat."

As she handed it over, a child's sour-tempered shout indicated to her exactly how the night was going to go.

"But I don't *want* to stay home with the stupid babysitter!"

Clearly, this was an ongoing debate. "Isn't that cute," Mark's wife, Linda, said with a laugh that was patronizing even to Sarah. "Remember, Billy, angel, you *like* Sarah...I know you want to go out with us, but Daddy and Mommy need some time to ourselves every once in a while..."

After escaping from the conversation in the kitchen, the lady of the house appeared and smiled brightly at Sarah. "Sarah! We're so grateful to you...Billy's just thrilled to see you again."

"No I'm not," said the petulant boy from the depths of the kitchen.

"Here's the number for Frank's Bistro." Mark thrust a piece of paper into Sarah's hand. "Don't hesitate to call and ask for us if you have any problems."

Sarah barely glanced at it. "Thanks. Say, uh—is there any way I could get paid now?"

"Sure! We'll pay you after we're back."

Sarah came dangerously close to saying, "Now means now," but had to wonder if these two would have even heard that much. As it stood, the Johnsons were already yanking on their coats.

"Billy knows his own schedule," said Linda, obliviously flipping her hair out of her coat and smiling as she took her husband's arm. "Feel free to do whatever he says! I'm sure it'll go fine."

"Uh," Sarah managed as Mark opened the door.

"We'll be back around eleven," Mr. Johnson assured her cheerily, ushering Linda out and waving at their hapless babysitter. "You kids have a good night, now!"

The door shut.

Sarah, now having achieved peak annoyance, stood staring at the front door with her hands on her hips. Something thumped behind her and she turned to find Billy standing at the edge of the living room... already in his pajamas, thankfully. One less pain.

"I'm hungry," said the boy.

"Hello to you, too."

"I said I'm *hungry,* Sarah!"

"Okay, Damien, sheesh, hold on—"

"Who's 'Damien?'"

"He's a character from a movie."

"And I'm like Damien?"

Biting back her smile lest the boy realize she was basically calling him the anti-Christ, Sarah said, "Uh-huh! You remind me a little of him, sometimes... Come on, let's get you settled in and fix you something to eat—"

After dropping her purse on the table by the couch, Sarah bent over the television to hit the power button.

Nothing happened except that the button made a limp clicking noise. The sound of a broken spring.

"Shi—shoot! Is this thing busted?"

"I broke it on Tuesday," said the boy. "I'm hungry, I want cereal."

"People in Hell want ice water," replied Sarah under her breath, trying the button a few more times to no avail. "Man! I guess you really *did* break it. Where's the remote?"

"Iunno," said the boy with a lame shrug, disappearing into the kitchen. "I'm going to get cereal!"

"Can you wait, please?"

"I can *do it* myself."

Damn! Somebody missed his nap, or something. Billy was usually an all right kid.

Sarah had to remind herself that the motorcycle was at stake here. She tried to keep her temper down.

"Okay," she said, sighing. "Sure, whatever. Just wait for me to help you with the milk, okay? Hold on...let me see if I can find the remote."

Sighing, shaking her head, Sarah wandered off. Though she grimaced at the clang of a bowl and the rattle of silverware, she refused to turn back around and so much as look in the kitchen.

That was what the kid wanted. Conflict. An excuse to make her out to be an unreasonable villain. Better to find that remote and put things to rest early on.

Now...how *was* she going to find that remote? The Johnson house had a way of turning her around. Its construction was somehow strange, with a lot of nooks and crannies, creepy laundry chutes down to the basement, and weird little rooms with strange connections that didn't always make sense. Not even the hallways seemed logical.

For instance, she first thought to check Mr. Johnson's office. Somehow, she found her way to the bathroom. Kind of unnerving: they were redoing the wallpaper in the bathroom, apparently. Sarah was startled to turn on the light and find no mirror on the wall.

Mark Johnson was always doing projects and leaving them half-finished—during her last shift, she had noticed a car in their garage. A dusty car. "It works now," Mark had said defensively when she inquired about it. "Just needs gas...and a bit of a tune-up, okay, sure! But it *does work.*"

Sure, Mr. Johnson. Okay. If Sarah didn't like the

couple so much, she probably wouldn't have tolerated them stiffing her. But the truth was that, despite their...quirks, the Johnsons were pretty nice people.

And, sure. Billy was all right, too. Even with everything considered.

Sarah assessed the mess before her: flashlights, torn wallpaper strips, new sample wallpapers, a first aid kit temporarily balanced upon the edge of the sink instead of its usual mount on the wall, plus other clutter that rendered the second bathroom mostly unusable. While she snooped, a clang echoed from the kitchen. Sarah grimaced at the sound of the boy saying, "Uh-oh."

"Be careful in there, please," she said above an impatient sigh, turning off the light with a glance to the shower on the other side of the guest bathroom.

Well, if they were going to renovate, maybe they'd get rid of that weird window over the shower.

She couldn't imagine living in the Johnson house and using the bathroom. Not even staying there as a guest struck her as a palatable idea. Just stepping in while looking for another room, Sarah felt as if she were being watched. Must have been the uncanny effect provoked by the missing mirror.

Or the house in general. Something about it felt 'off' to her. She told herself that this was all due to her imagination and the sanitarium break-out... But it was the little details.

The vintage monster movie posters in Mr. Johnson's office, for instance. They weren't creepy in and of themselves, being from cheesy movies—black-and-white features that she could have now watched any night on *Elvira's Movie Macabre.* But in that house, peering at Sarah even before she flipped on the office's light, the posters had a way of adding to the unpleasant atmosphere.

More watchers—more eyes on her as she wandered around the perimeter of the room in search of the remote, glanced briefly over the books, looked boredly at the VHS recorder, hit 'play' and 'pause' as the result of an almost childish compulsion.

Yes, she was being childish. Nervous for no reason. She'd babysat millions of times before. Nothing was going to go wrong, unless she got back to the kitchen to discover Billy had upended the milk jug. At this rate, teaching herself how to fix the broken power button would have been faster than finding the remote.

One last wrong door opened up to a pleasant second-floor den with a turntable...and a towering antique liquor cabinet, tempting with its glass doors. And, she discovered with a frown, locked. No extra reimbursement, then...well, maybe she'd look for the key when she had a chance.

The remote turned out to be stowed in Billy's room, of course. Man, kids were always doing stuff like this! Now stewing in annoyance, Sarah clomped down the stairs.

She was so irritated that she barely avoided nailing her shin on the squat shelf of children's books inconveniently placed beside the landing. Sarah shot it a hateful glance while she rounded the corner in to the living room.

Bookshelf forgotten, she waved the remote. "Hey, you twerp! You could have told me it was in your room!"

"I forgot," said the kid lamely, adding, "and I spilled some milk," while Sarah was in the middle of hitting the power button.

"Man! Just sit down." The irritated girl set the remote firmly down upon the television and didn't even glance at the screen. She turned away while the kid hurried to his seat on the floor approximately six inches in front of it.

"You're going to hurt your eyes looking at that so close," she told him before heading into the kitchen to see the damage.

Ugh! Were you kidding her with this? Somehow, in pouring milk into the cereal bowl, Billy had managed to drip it all down the side of the counter. "Okay," she called over her shoulder, "no more kitchen privileges for you, dude. Next time, you have to wait for me."

"Aw! Come on, Sarah! It was an accident."

Grumbling under her breath, Sarah tromped to the sink, tore a few paper towels off the roll, then got down on her hands and knees to clean the worst of it. While she wiped up the side of the sink, Sarah leapt in place: the phone on the kitchen wall had rung out at a tone so abrupt, so shrill, that it frightened her.

"Jeez, Sarah." The babysitter shook her head as she pushed off of the sink to clamber to her feet.

With one hand braced against the counter she still idly wiped, Sarah used the other to pick up the phone and said in a tone that was intended to telegraph mild annoyance at the interruption, "Johnson residence."

Nothing. Empty line. Open space in her ear.

"Hello?"

No sound. Nothing at all.

Except—was that somebody breathing?

Sarah's still-wiping hand at last paused. "Is somebody there?"

Mumbling.

Eyes narrowed, Sarah tried to discern the words. It was like listening to somebody ramble under their breath. The kind of externalized inner dialogue most people kept to themselves, but that certain types of mentally ill people just couldn't contain.

"I'm sorry," said Sarah finally, looking for any excuse to hang up the phone. "I can't seem to hear you... you're going to have to call—"

"Don't lie."

The man's voice was so sharp, so deep, that it was monstrous somehow. Confused, Sarah could only manage, "Excuse me?"

"Don't lie," repeated the caller. "The game is up."

Sarah's blood ran cold. She glanced over her shoulder to the dark window overlooking the back yard.

Her own reflection peered back, the kitchen lighting rendering the Johnson's garden shed invisible from inside the house.

Keeping her tone pleasant and polite as possible, Sarah tried to wrap things up before they got weirder. "I'm sorry. I think there must be some kind of—"

"The demons drag my legs to hell! While you sit in your ivory tower..."

Sarah was so startled that she couldn't have managed a response even if such a sentence were the sort of thing one expected a response to.

The caller went on, his hard tone so crisp it might as well have been straight in her ear. A voice in her head. Her own heart, slamming in her body.

"Don't you judge me," warned the caller at last. "I see all."

The line died in Sarah's hand.

5.

THE HUGO household clamored while its invader hung up the phone. Mostly, that clamor was a series of gurgling, muted cries—screams against duct tape and makeshift gags of old rope found in the garage.

Amazing they could still scream. Mr. and Mrs. Hugo had been trapped with their child's dead body at their feet for most of the day. The corpse was starting to smell.

While the couple wept and the domicile, as much a captive as they, served as the only witness to their suffering, the killer yanked the phone from the outlet. He tossed it against the wall with a theatrical shatter of plastic casing and metal interior audible from rooms away.

"Please," gasped Mrs. Hugo as the murderer stormed back into the bedroom where they were being kept. Mr. Hugo, still bound to his chair, had toppled over while trying to edge steadily toward the bedroom's only exit. The huge monster in their house bent over and set him effortlessly upright without a word. He was considering getting a knife out of their kitchen when it happened.

The doorbell rang.

Mrs. Hugo, who had somehow managed to get the gag out of her drooling mouth well enough to speak, gasped. "That's my sister—that's what we've been trying to tell you all day. Please! You don't want to be here when she comes in, do you? You don't want her to see you. What if she saw your face? Then she'd be able to tell the police that it was you who—who did this."

Big tears flowed down the woman's cheeks while the doorbell rang another time.

"You could just go. Please, just go. We'll never tell anybody what happened! We'll think of something to tell the police about our son. Something, anything. Just don't hurt us—no! Wait! Don't hurt my sister, either—"

The killer's long strides carried him briskly out of the room.

Mrs. Hugo's heartbeat seemed to hammer throughout the very house—seemed to echo off the walls and back into her ears.

Oh, what if she had a heart attack? That would have been just like her. Having a heart attack while a murderer was in her house. Hah! It would have been almost funny. Yes, almost…somehow.

The doorbell rang a third time. Mrs. Hugo grew sicker by the second as she wondered whether she'd left the sliding glass door unlocked.

Yes—yes, of course, she had. That was how the man had gotten in, after all. He'd simply let himself in while the family got ready for the day.

Mrs. Hugo had been in the kitchen. She'd exited to the adjacent laundry room and got her linens from the dryer. When she'd turned back around and re-entered the kitchen.

There he was.

Oh, she'd heard the sliding glass door, of course. The thing was old, off its track, made a terrible grind when you opened it. She'd had a warning, then. She just hadn't listened, confident it was only her husband coming back in from looking across the garden. Instead she found the man who would end both their lives.

"She's going to try the back door," whispered Mrs. Hugo to her husband, shutting her eyes against the agony of knowing that her sister was about to walk into certain death. "Oh, Anthony! She's going to try to come in through the back."

To think! All those fights she had her sister gotten into, all because Catherine kept letting herself into the house.

Maybe Mrs. Hugo had been in the right after all.

To think she'd ever doubted herself and her right to privacy! To think...this was how it was going to end.

Her chest heaved with the sobs she struggled to repress. Sure enough, the familiar clatter of the house's side gate reverberated through the architecture's walls.

While Mrs. Hugo exchanged a glance with her muted husband, she tried one last futile time to work her wrists out of her binds.

"Do you hear him?" Her voice was a whisper to her husband as she begged to know, "Can you hear where he's gone?"

Anthony Hugo shook his head, eyes grim and dark after the day-long ordeal that left his only son dead at his feet. Mrs. Hugo inhaled, exhaled, nodded, braced herself.

Off on the other side of the house, the poorly aligned sliding glass door opened with a noise like a scream of agony. "Hello! Erica? Anthony? It's Catherine! He—hello?"

She had no choice. She had to save her sister's life—had to do anything. After all, strapped to a chair as she was, Mrs. Hugo was already doomed. No reason for her sister to risk her life when that result wasn't likely to be changed.

Gasping great lungfuls of air, Erica screamed, "Catherine! Get out! Turn around! Turn around and get help!"

"What was that?"

Mrs. Hugo threw back her head and sobbed in frustration at her sister. Catherine had an incredible ear for all matters of gossip, but naturally couldn't be relied upon to listen at the most vital of moments.

Catherine's footsteps carried lightly through the house as she made her way to the bedroom. Mrs. Hugo almost couldn't bring herself to look, but realized this was going to be the last time she would ever see her sister. Erica forced herself to open her eyes when Catherine appeared in the doorway.

The more welcome of the Hugos' two guests took in the room. Her face fell. "Why—Erica, Tony, what—oh! God"—now she saw the boy and stepped forward, then back—"what's happened?"

"You need to run, Catherine—run and—no!"

Too late. Much too late.

The elongated blade of the boning knife looked so alien after penetrating through her sister that Mrs. Hugo didn't recognize it at first. Not while it was covered in blood so red it seemed black in the low light of the house.

Her sister shared her surprise, mouth opening in a cry that was more a short noise signifying astonishment than a scream of mortal agony. While the knife slid out and blood pumped from her new chest wound, the killer put a hand on the back of her head. He simply pushed.

Catherine toppled face-first upon the floor and Burr stooped over her in an instant. Mrs. Hugo and her husband were a captive, wild-eyed, screaming audience as the mad man stabbed Catherine again and again, puncturing through the flesh of her back so many times that if anyone had kept count they would have swiftly lost track.

Soon the act somehow abstracted itself. The meaning was lost and Mrs. Hugo's screaming calmed to a kind of hyperventilation. Wet sobs still hiccuped up from her chest from time to time, but, for the most part, the depth of her horror died with her sister.

Being forced to sit with her son's corpse for so long hadn't been enough. It hadn't been proof of her fate like this. But, seeing her sister's blood spread out across the floor, everything was made quite clear to Mrs. Hugo.

This really *was* how she was going to die. Not in a car accident, or of an illness, or in her sleep when she was well advanced in age. No. She was going to die here, amid the bloodstained tatters of her suburban life: her child already dead at her feet, the only question remaining one of whether her husband would go first or second.

First, it seemed. She couldn't have explained it, but she knew as soon as the killer sat back on his haunches and locked eyes with her. He wanted to—*save* her, maybe.

It was a thought so matter-of-fact amid her state of shock that she didn't realize how chilling the notion would have been any other time. How hideous it was to be left for last, like the final few bites of the best part of a meal.

But there was no touching her now. Not her mind. It was so strange! That clarity, that coldness. What else could she do, though? Her hands were literally tied.

Her husband didn't seem to share her sudden lamblike acceptance. As the criminal stepped over the pool of blood and closed the distance between them, Anthony's struggles doubled in intensity. His shoulders jerked, his body writhed in his seat. Mrs. Hugo watched impassively and tried not to think of her husband as a coward in his final moments.

Was that a cruel thought to have? She had to be cruel. Had to dissever herself from him, along with the rest of the world she would soon be leaving. The killer, having jammed the knife down into Tony's eye and through the brain beyond, worked the blade back and forth. A massive seizure twitched his body as a result of the trauma, and Mrs. Hugo felt nothing.

Nothing.

The only feeling left was the severe nausea produced by the gore that spilled from her husband's open face.

Such horrible things could happen in this world! Such terrible sights. From that perspective, Mrs. Hugo wasn't sad to leave it behind. This hideous moment was just one last thing. One last disgusting trial to endure before she needed endure no more. Then she would be with her husband, her child, her sister.

The killer turned on her. The knife dripped with her husband's gray matter. Not so gray beneath its coating of vivid crimson.

Mrs. Hugo forced herself to meet his eyes. She stared in defiance. She waited.

The killer let the knife clatter to the floor. She expected him to say something, anything at last.

He didn't.

He turned around and left the room.

All her bravery flowed out of her. All her acceptance vanished in a second.

Incredible—with a renewed hope of survival, fear was reborn again. Fear, that most powerful of all survival instincts, was perhaps the result of desperation. The result of failure again becoming only a potential, rather than the guarantee it had seemed mere seconds before.

Why had he done this? Had he left this knife for her to use? This was all part of his game to him, she was sure, but...God, there really was a chance now, wasn't there?

If only—if only she could just get down to it.

Erica strained to listen for the killer's footsteps, but couldn't determine if he'd exited through the sliding glass door. Had her sister been given time to close it behind her? If so, she would have heard it squeal shut, then open again when the killer left.

But...did it even matter if he was still in the house?

Mrs. Hugo had to keep trying. Erica had to keep trying.

Clenching her teeth, Erica threw herself down sideways. She had to bite back a sob as her face landed inches from her dead son's. The shock and bitter betrayal of life against him was so plain in his corpse's face that she had to look away rather than ruminate on it a second longer.

Instead, her elbow working in unison with her hip and her weight rocking back and forth, Erica managed to get her back to the knife. Slowly, carefully, amid a lot of blind groping, her fingers brushed the cool, wet handle.

Okay! Okay, great.

Holding her breath, Erica struggled for a better grip, then grimaced as the blade bobbed up against her forearm.

The killer had picked the longest knife in the kitchen. It was, to say the least, unwieldy to use from a position like this. Hands bound behind her back. To use it to free herself from such a bind was nearly impossible. Certainly impossible without injury.

But these were desperate times. Erica had to do whatever it took to get herself out of danger and into the arms of the law.

Yes—she had to do whatever she could to get herself up. Out of this chair. Out of this house.

Far, far away.

Though she jabbed herself three times with the

blade, she realized she was bleeding only when she found the handle slipperier than it had been before. While it slid from her hand and jammed up against her wrist, she hissed, wiggled her arms back, worked to reclaim her blind grip on the knife—

And to her good fortune, the duct tape, already worn through, at last tore.

Gasping, Erica wiggled her wrists victoriously back and forth.

Oh, yes! Yes, that was it! Just a little more…

Perfect! The two halves of duct tape separated.

Free! Erica was free!

Joy filled her. She was so happy that she almost laughed, but laughing and attracting him back with that laughter was an idea that terrified her. Even so, giddy enough that she no longer saw the corpses of her family, Erica sprang upright and rubbed her wrists. Then, body low, she made her way out of the room.

She hadn't cleared the threshold into the hallway by the time the man, waiting for her outside the door all that time, snatched her by the bleeding wrist with one hand. His other massive fist grabbed her neck.

Soon both hands were at her throat.

Erica gasped, eyes widening in fresh terror as he squeezed.

He wanted me to be afraid, she realized as, amid the buzz of asphyxiation, encroaching darkness obscured the face of her murderer. *He let me think I had a chance to flee because he saw that I wasn't afraid anymore...this bastard wanted me to have hope again.*

Erica might have been impressed by Burr's dedication to misanthropy if she hadn't died seconds later.

6.

WELL, THAT was disturbing.

Sarah tried not to let the phone call rattle her...but with everything going on around the town, how could she avoid it? She liked to consider herself, if nothing else, a brave person. The general atmosphere of the past few days was clearly starting to get to her.

Maybe she just needed to be a little more rational. The call had to be some kind of prank—yes, a prank. But by whom?

Somebody who knew she'd be at the Johnson's. Somebody who knew she'd be alone. There was only one person who knew all that. Sarah rolled her eyes while dialing Jill's number, preemptively annoyed even before her friend picked up the phone with a brusque, "Hello?"

"Hey, it's Sarah."

"Sarah, who?"

"Shut up, bitch." While Jill responded to this with an asinine laugh, Sarah rolled her eyes. "Where do you get off? Freaking me out with bogus calls like that—what a jerk move!"

"What do you mean?"

"Your phone mumbling bullshit just now—you scared the hell out of me, dude. I mean, good job, I guess, but—"

"I have literally no idea what you're talking about. 'Phone mumbling,' what now?"

Maybe it wasn't Jill. Stomach twisting at the notion that her friend had nothing to do with the prank, Sarah leaned back against the wall and said, "Forget about it—I guess it was just a wrong number, or something."

"Bitch, you're paranoid as hell. Why don't you call Jack and get him to come over to protect you?"

"I can't just invite a random guy to somebody else's house! Why don't *you* just come over? It's super spooky here."

"Aw, poor baby! Do you need me to bring your blankie and your bottle with me, too?"

"Okay, you know what? Never mind, stay home."

"God, I'm kidding! Lighten up—sure, I'll come over. Be there in ten?"

"Please, thank you." Sighing in relief, Sarah recited the address and said, "I'm sorry, I know it's stupid. That phone call really rattled me."

"Whatever, loser! I love you, anyway. See you soon."

The call ended and Sarah hung up the receiver. What a moron she was being! She couldn't believe her own anxiety. Jill was right to tease her. It was a nice night outside—and, inside, Billy had even started to clean up his act.

Though...when Sarah came to collect the empty cereal bowl from him, she frowned. The scene on the television depicted a few ghouls stooped over the black-and-white grass of a farmhouse yard.

While they gnawed away on the mottled flesh still attached to large bones clutched in their blood- and meat-smeared hands, Sarah glanced at Billy's mesmerized face. "Should you be watching this?"

"You were the one who put it on!"

"Yeah, but I was distracted—is this *Night of the Living Dead?* Dude, you're way too young for—"

"No! Come on, Sarah!" She had been reaching for the remote but the boy lurched forward like one of the film's own zombies. Tone urgent, he grabbed the hem of her shirt. "Mom and Dad let me watch whatever I want before bedtime."

Yeah, well. Billy's parents seemed to let him do a lot of things that Sarah personally wouldn't have...but they were the parents, she guessed. Shrugging, shaking her head, Sarah said, "Whatever. When you're having nightmares all night because of this, don't come crying to me about it."

And anyway, it was a good distraction for him.

Sarah had a mission now. If she was going to have Jill over and feel anything other than lame about it, she'd might as well try to make it fun. That liquor cabinet had been pretty tempting...but the question was, where did the Johnsons keep their key?

Wherever Billy couldn't find it, was probably the answer. The kid was beyond precocious—he was a trouble-maker. He was going to grow up to be one, anyway. That was why Sarah liked him, probably...he reminded her of herself.

So...if Sarah were a kid Billy's age, and her parents hid a key from her, where would they put it? The bedroom? Hm...no, probably her dad's office. Better check both.

Ensuring the boy was occupied with the gory movie, Sarah moved in silence through the eerie Johnson house. She soon found herself once more in that in-renovation bathroom.

After trying out the flashlights and discovering one was conveniently sized for a pocket, Sarah selected it, made it at home in the fabric of her gold- and white-striped shirt, then crept to the master bedroom. Mrs. Johnson kept a neat bedroom and Sarah therefore avoided touching anything unnecessarily, but she did peer into the night stand drawers and blush a little at the contents.

No key, though.

What was in this cabinet against the wall? She tried it, frowning, and found it locked. A gun cabinet, maybe? Now that she thought about it, Mr. Johnson had talked once about going shooting from time to time. Yikes! That was one cabinet she was fine with keeping locked...

Figuring the liquor cabinet key had to be elsewhere, she doubled back to have a second look at the office.

Hm...nothing stuck to the underside of the desk, which was her dad's old trick. Junk in one drawer, files in another, Mrs. Johnson's craft supplies stored haphazardly in a third for want of a better space.

They needed to get some storage space arranged in their house...for a place with so many weird closets and strange turns, there wasn't really an organizational system to speak of. She even found a VHS on the bookshelf of another room while on her hunt for the key. It was tempting to put the movie back where it belonged, but then the Johnsons might have gotten the impression that Sarah was snooping. Couldn't have that, after all!

Sarah was on her way downstairs again when the beam of the flashlight caught it. No, not the liquor cabinet key, though for a moment the metallic sparkle gave her an inner glimmer of hope.

Instead, the flashlight had illuminated something wedged behind the small bookshelf at the base of the stairs.

With a frown and a glance toward the artificial movie screams from the adjacent living room, Sarah knelt to push aside the small children's bookshelf.

Filled with little more than picture books and thin novelettes as it was, the blue shelf was easy to move. It scooted a few feet to the right without a problem and Sarah marveled at the thick line of dust between it and the wall. This shelf must have been put here when the Johnsons moved in...and she could see why.

The shelf, it turned out, concealed a tiny door.

Man! Sarah hated tiny doors like this one. Boiler room doors, furnace doors, attic doors. Even laundry chutes spooked her, and the Johnsons' house had a couple of those. Sarah supposed it followed logically that a house with creepy little laundry chutes would also, somewhere, have a creepy little door.

As a small child—say, Billy's age—she'd always felt something horrible, some small and crippled thing, lay in wait behind tiny doors. They seemed to house the sorts of things that came out only at night, when nobody was there to watch them emerge from their dens.

No question, tiny doors freaked Sarah out...but she had to admit that they sparked her insatiable inner sense of curiosity.

Okay—so, maybe she was a little nosy. Was that really such a crime?

And, well, it wasn't like the liquor cabinet key was going to be in *there*...but, if she didn't settle her mind by checking, the question of what lay on the other side of that little door was going to plague her through the night.

With one last glance toward the living room, Sarah tried the knob of the squat door. It was unlocked. The babysitter bent down to stick her head, along with the flashlight, inside the dark crawlspace.

The vacant face staring back into hers was so hideous that she screamed.

7.

THE TOWN was transforming—no doubt about it.

Quiet suburbs were no longer so quiet. Quiet neighborhoods now overflowed with screams. Quiet houses ran red with blood, their clean floors filthy with the remains of human beings.

Quiet streets were host to the fast-moving, broad strides of Neoklaus Burr, who made his steady way down asphalt paths. His instincts were devoted to one goal.

Two goals. One goal, in service to the other, was the goal of remaining unseen.

To stay out of sight, Burr moved mostly through back yards and drainage ditches. These unwilling strips of land served him well until he stole behind a fence while a fleet of cop cars sped past. The caravan resembled, in so many ways, the parades that were better fits for the small town's quiet roads: lights flashing, sirens blaring, an ambulance and television news van both in hot pursuit. The whole procession lacked only a parade float...or maybe a hearse.

Satisfied that the cops had missed him, Burr now risked taking a street. The concrete sidewalk was faster than the obstacle course presented by creeping through yard on yard, and if he kept his head low, no one would recognize him. He should have checked the house he'd just left for a stocking cap or other head covering. If only he had something to hide his face behind!

Yes, if only. If he'd had such a thing, the already devastated town would not have witnessed yet another death.

Vernon Brown was a prime example of a man with community concern. He had to be—after all, Vernon was a family man. The community was his children's community before it was his, and he had to make sure it was safe for them.

Therefore, Vernon was a very vigilant citizen, and his time as a green beret made him confident that if anyone could maintain a one-man neighborhood watch, it was him. The big German shepherd he'd trained to follow his every command, practically before he thought it, only added to his comfort.

All this was to say that Vernon never thought twice about walking at night. No, not even after a sanitarium break-out. In fact, he sort of daydreamed about encountering the bastard. Wouldn't that be righteous? Yeah, hell yeah! Just try to start a fight and see what happens, lunatic.

That was what Vernon told himself all day. All evening, too. His wife had listened boredly while, watching the news of the dead jogger, Vern assured her, "If that guy met me and Titus here"—the dog panted happily while he patted its head—"we'd give him a couple of things to think about while he waited for the cops to come collect him...in fact, he'd probably be begging for 'em to show up! Huh, boy? Ain't that right, Titus?"

Somewhere along the line, his attention had shifted from his wife to his dog. Maybe this was because the dog was much more interested in what Vern had to say.

"That's nice, dear," said his wife, barely looking up from her TV dinner even as she went on to tell the kids, "Come on, now. If you guys don't finish the vegetables, I'm not even going to bother with that Mrs. Smith's pie you were all excited about before..."

Having finished his own tray of microwaved food, Vernon dusted off his hands and grinned down at his dog. "You ready, boy?"

That was all Titus needed. At his human's question, the dog sprang up to dash across the living room floor. There he circled, prancing a few excited times around the foyer tiles before sitting neatly upon his haunches. "What a good boy," enthused Vernon with a chuckle. "And so smart! Dog's smarter than me."

"Practically Lassie," agreed his wife. Her eyes finally lifted not to her husband but to her television's screen. "Don't lose any fights while you're out there..."

"Hah! As if that's even possible. Why, I really do wish that jerk would try it—yeah, then we'll see—"

A few minutes later master and dog both enjoyed the crisp night air. Was there anything quite like the freedom of the neighborhood after dark? Ah, yeah! Vern always felt it was like having the whole world to himself.

Especially with this curfew. Boy, it made everything weird. Very quiet. Sure, it was always a quiet neighborhood...but now hardly anybody was out. There were definitely no kids playing, and you could usually find at least one or two trying to squeeze in a few extra minutes after dark.

Maybe that was why Vernon had such a funny burst of intuition while seeing the guy from a block away.

There were other indications, more obvious or logical ones, outside of the hairs that rose on the back of his neck. Who else was going to be out on a night like tonight, after all? Vern had a *reason* to be outside. He was walking his dog.

This guy didn't have a dog. This guy didn't have nothing but a red boiler suit of some kind, old and faded and somehow ill-fitting. Like this guy, who was already huge, had once been even huger. Like this guy maybe spent some time incarcerated.

Like…maybe he hadn't had as many opportunities to move around, because he spent so much of his time medicated in a cell.

Vernon narrowed his eyes through the dark. He tried to make out this guy's face. That family killer's mugshot had been plastered all over the news all day long.

If it really was the guy, Vern would be able to tell when he was a little closer…and by then he'd have to be ready to make a decision. Had he brought his utility knife? Vern tapped his pocket. Yeah, it was there.

But would he even have time to take it out and get it open? Boy, this guy moved fast! Huge legs, big steps, fast strides.

Something about the motion clearly unnerved Titus. The dog's low growl rumbled from its muzzle as the men grew nearer. The noise raised to a bark when the huge guy was about twenty feet away, and by that point Vern's hand was in his pocket for the knife.

Somehow, even that was too late. At the dog's bark, the guy looked up. Oh, yeah. Years older, paler from spending so long in a crazy ward: but that was the child-killing son-of-a-bitch, all right.

"Hey," shouted Vern, chest puffing up. The green beret expected the man to stop.

He didn't.

"Hey," Vern shouted again while the dark barked on, "what's your name?"

Ten feet separated them now.

"You don't have to tell me. Burr, right?"

Five feet.

Titus whined sharply. At once the dog spun on his heels and dashed back home as fast as he could. The leash jerked out of Vernon's unready hand and he cried, "Hey—Titus!"

Thrown off-balance, looking back toward the dog as he was, Vernon was completely unprepared for Burr to grab his shoulder with one han. By the time Vern looked back at him, the killer's other hand had raised the D-cell flashlight taken off the body of Aaron Parsons.

On the first impact of the hard metal flashlight against the top of his skull, Vern made a noise like a gag. That was the sound of him biting off his own tongue and being subject to the inundation of blood that flowed into his mouth upon the forceful clamp of his jaw.

The green beret stumbled forward in astonishment. Burr grabbed him by the front of the shirt and used the flashlight to cave his teeth in.

Blood, along with fragments of bone and chunks of red tissue, flew in all directions. Vernon sobbed against the pain—more wretchedly, it was perhaps worth mentioning, than had Mrs. Hugo or even Burr's confused wife all those decades before. Oblivious to this suffering, Burr used one hand to squeeze open the emptied cavity of the green beret's mouth.

Of course, to Neoklaus Burr, Vernon wasn't a green

beret. He wasn't even Vernon. Not even a 'he,' really. Vernon had been reduced far past his humanity, perhaps because Burr was himself so monstrous. No one with whom he interacted could long maintain many of their own traces of whatever it was that made a human distinct from the other animals in the world.

After peering down into the blood-coated throat of his victim, Burr turned the flashlight around. He jammed it handle-first into the gaping black and red orifice. Vernon had already been drowning on his own blood, but the new gurgle of more immediate suffocation was distinct even from that. Confident the stranger was seconds from death, Burr released his grip of the body and let it drop to his feet.

The captive streets could not intervene as Burr bent and searched the still struggling corpse's pockets. He thought about taking the knife but it was such a useless little thing that instead he stuck it into the dying man's left eye as life faded from the right.

Blood surged out over the idiot's face and oozed down his cheekbone. Burr would have left it at that, but, at the police sirens again rising in the distance, he twisted the blade to add insult to injury.

This was just for his own gratification. By now Vernon was completely dead.

Then, long before the cruisers were ever visible to the killer, Burr darted down the fence line dividing the two nearest houses. He learned from his mistake. He began to again make his way through back yards.

Had to double back a little before he made new progress, though. Let the cops deal with the dog walker...and these cops had to come from somewhere. Nearest place they'd just been? The last house where Burr had killed, of course.

If he'd been a betting man—if he'd been any kind of man at all, instead of a homicidal monster—Burr would have guessed the investigators would have dropped everything to respond to a phone call that so much as reported a firecracker going off.

The sounds of a man being beaten to death in the middle of the sidewalk?

No wonder they were rushing to the latest crime scene in hopes of apprehending the killer. No wonder they left the previous one undefended.

So, that was Burr's destination. That last house. Maybe he could steal a car now that there would be fewer cops on the road. All of the small town officers had clustered together. It made them easy to avoid. The car in the garage of the house where he'd spent the day seemed a logical choice. What had been the family's name?

Oh—'Hugo.' Burr heard a reporter say the name into a camera poised in front of the pitifully taped-off crime scene. The paramedics had already driven off. The only ones left at the scene were that reporter, his camera man, and the big white van conveniently parked along the side of the road.

"Little is known about the state of the crime scene,"

the oblivious reporter rambled, "as officers have for-
bidden our entry. However, from what we've been
able to glean of this developing tragedy, all members of the Hugo residence had been dead for several
hours prior to police response..."

8.

SARAH GRIPPED her chest, breathless amid the rapid hammer of her heart. Suspended a few inches from her face, the clown mask seemed to laugh at her terror.

Yeah, real funny! Who kept a creepy mask like this in a hidden crawlspace, anyway?

Billy called without getting up, "Are you okay?"

Sarah stuck her head out from the cramped door.

"Yeah," she said, "don't worry. I'm fine."

Back in the dark of the crawlspace, she ran her flashlight's beam over the old plastic mask and scowled. Was this the previous homeowner's idea of a prank?

Sarah thought about tearing the mask down, but the beam reflected off of something else. A dull shine at the edge of the light.

With a sidelong glance at the creepy mask and a sigh for the cramped space, Sarah cursed her curiosity. She twisted in a little farther to see what it was she was even looking at.

A kitchen knife.

Weird. Very weird. She wasn't sure why her hands went numb at the sight—no more than she was sure why she had to tighten her grip on the flashlight to keep its aim true.

What was a knife doing in a crawlspace like this? The Johnsons hadn't put it here, that was certain.

In fact, going by the sheer level of dust coating its blade, the knife had been there far longer than the bookshelf.

Sarah had to wonder if the previous owners had even known about it. Maybe it was from owners before that—the people who had built the house. The plastic of the mask looked old and degraded, brittle from the onslaught of time. And as for the knife…

Covered in rust.

A thick layer of brown corrosion obscured so much of the silver blade that it was amazing Sarah had seen it at all, even in the flashlight beam. Frowning, she once again considered taking down the mask to throw it away along with the old knife.

But, well…Sarah wasn't exactly eager to touch either item and disturb, say, a colony of spiders that happened to be nesting underneath. Deciding it was better for her to forget the whole thing, Sarah wiggled back out and shrieked again to find Billy standing over her.

The boy was too curious to care that he had startled her, which he no doubt would have found hilarious under normal circumstances. "What are you looking for?"

"God! Billy! Don't freak me out like that!"

"Sorry—what are you looking for, though?"

"Oh, uh, the fuse box. Just, like, for emergencies, you know."

"That's in the garage! I watched Dad use it one time. You want me to show you?"

"Uh, you know what? Not right now, but—hey, Billy, uh—do you know anything about a clown mask? Like, did you ever get one for Christmas? A birthday?"

"A clown mask?" The boy hummed and shook his head. "I don't think so. I don't like clowns."

"Yeah...me neither."

Sarah shut the tiny door again. She would have moved the bookshelf right back, but Jill's familiar shave-and-a-haircut knock pattern rang out on the front door.

Billy dashed for it before she could stop him. "I'll get it!"

"Hey! Get back here, you're in your pajamas! Why don't you go ahead and go to bed, Billy?"

"But I'm not tired!"

Annoyed, Sarah said, "Well—then go watch your zombie movie." Another knock. She waved him off

71

imperiously, saying, "Just let grown-ups answer the door, okay, buddy?"

Only as she opened that door herself did Sarah realize she should have checked the peephole first. Seeing Jill's smiling face, though, Sarah dismissed the fear. What was she worried about? Did she think she was so special that this house, of all houses in town, would be the one to attract the killer?

"Hey, scaredy-cat!" Jill stepped past Sarah, adding with a grin, "Uh-oh! And this must be *Billy*. What's going on, little dude?"

The boy still hovered on the edge of the living room. "Who's that?"

"This is just my friend, Jill. She's, uh—"

"Sarah got all freaked out because it's the spooky month," said Jill. Sarah was relieved that her friend was good enough with kids to whitewash over the whole 'lunatic escaped from the asylum' situation making all the grown-ups so paranoid. "So I came over to keep her company for awhile. Is that cool with you?"

Her explanation seemed to please the boy even more than did being asked permission for the visit. "Sarah's a big old chicken," he crowed in delight. "She wanted me to turn off my movie because it was scaring her, but it's just a goofy story! Zombies aren't real, anyway."

"Oh, zombies? I love zombies, what movie are you watching? *Night of the Living Dead?* I love that one...

imagine being stuck in a house in the middle of no-where like that! The people in that movie are worse than the monsters..."

Seeing a potential kindred spirit, the boy asked, "Do you want to see my zombie figures?"

Bless Jill and her tact! If only she were as under-standing with her peers. "Hey, cool idea! But maybe you should show them to me some other time...I think Sarah's had her fill of the undead tonight, right?"

"Totally," said Sarah with a roll of her eyes and a grateful sigh for her friend. "Sorry, Billy. You go enjoy the movie without us, okay?"

While the boy trotted off, Sarah told her friend with real gratitude, "Thanks for coming, dude."

"Oh, for sure! Anytime. Plus—well."

Jill glanced around to make sure Billy was out of earshot and nonetheless lowered her voice while say-ing, "I know you told me the addy before, and I knew I recognized the street...but, like, I didn't realize this was *the* house. No wonder you're all freaked out!"

Sarah's brow furrowed. "What do you mean?"

"Shit, dude—"

Sarah sharply hushed her friend's foul mouth.

Wincing, Jill glanced toward the living room. "Ugh, sorry...is there someplace grown-ups can talk?"

A couple of minutes later, Sarah and Jill had made themselves comfortable in the upstairs den. Before Jill could get too excited about the heavy antique li-quor cabinet, Sarah revealed that its glass doors were sadly locked. Instead Jill busied herself by thumbing through the Johnsons' record collection. Sarah asked, "So, what were you talking about?"

"*Well...*I'm just surprised that you didn't know about this place. The guy who lived here came home one day—this was in, like, 1960 or something—and totally murdered his wife and kids."

Sarah's eyes widened. "What? Why?"

"Do I look like a psychiatrist? I don't freaking know...it was just *brutal*, though. Like, mega warped. I guess he walked in and started stabbing his wife, and then he killed his daughter and his baby while the cops were on the way."

"The *baby?*"

"Straight up. Not only that, but he *ate* it." While Sarah felt herself pale, her stomach churning at the heinous thought, Jill's eyebrows lifted. "You think a dude who kills his wife and daughter is going to let a baby live? Like, come on. People get fucked in the head."

"I guess—just, eating it? I mean, what the fuck."

"Dude has problems."

"But, like, they found him, right?"

"Oh, yeah...they found him. They caught him right after he killed the baby and once he was convicted the court locked him away—in Monroe State."

As Sarah's chilling understanding of what was being expressed to her slowly swept over her head, Jill's dynamic eyebrows wiggled in inappropriate enthusiasm. "You want to guess what his freaking name was?"

"Burr," whispered Sarah, flashing back to her conversation with Jack. Then, with an even more violent twist of her guts, the strange phone call.

"That's right, dude. This used to be Neoklaus Burr's house. This isn't just any old murder house... it's the murder house of the guy who broke out of the sanitarium yesterday."

In retrospect, Sarah should have gotten up, called Frank's Bistro right then, and forced the Johnson's to come back early. Yes, she should have...but if she had, what would have happened to the Johnsons?

It was better, then, that Sarah had to put on a brave face or risk the merciless teasing of her friend; better that she should have gone through all she was doomed to go through that night.

If the only other alternative was knowing the Johnsons had died in the pattern of the Burr family, then Sarah would have done it all again a thousand times.

"You're just trying to freak me out," said Sarah, at that moment oblivious to the dark night ahead of her. Jill's arch look said it all.

"Believe what you want," Jill said, drawing an Ornette Coleman vinyl from the collection. "Why is this sleeve all wonky on the end? Hey—"

Jill had spread the cardboard with her fingers to peer inside. Now she flipped the record over to give it a shake.

A small pair of keys slid out upon the turntable.

The sorts of small, easily lost keys designed for a safe...or a liquor cabinet.

"Of course!" Sarah sat up with a gasp of delight while Jill laughed. More grateful than ever for her friend, the designated babysitter continued, "I knew they had to be keeping it somewhere weird. And what kid is going to look through their parents' jazz albums?"

"Like, duh! Hold on, hold on..." Producing a drum-roll noise with her mouth, Jill sprang across the den and made sure Sarah watched while she slid the key into the tiny lock.

"Hold on," Jill urged her again, turning it until it clicked and cheering when it did. "Ta-da!"

Sarah buried her face in her hands, relieved. "Oh my God! *Yes.*"

"See, dude? You just needed me around..." Wearing an ear-to-ear grin, Jill opened the glass front of the cabinet and removed a tumbler of amber whiskey from the shelf inside. "All right! We've got the drinks and—*some* tunes, even if they're old ones. Now if we just had some guys it would be a party. Do you have Jack's number?"

Still uncertain about the whole thing, Sarah glanced at the shut door of the den. "I don't know, Jill...if Billy tells his parents, I mean, I could lose this gig."

"Oh, whatever! They didn't even pay you last time, did they? So there's already, like, a 50-50 chance they're going to stiff you again...you'd might as well have fun."

Tongue running over her dry lips, Sarah began, "Man—"

"No! Quit it!"

Sarah jolted in surprise at Jill's indignant shout. She paid her friend closer attention.

One hand on her hip, Jill went on, "Stop making excuses! You really *are* such a scaredy-cat. Come on, you know you want him to come over here. Nothing's going to happen between you two tonight. And if you're worried it will, then I'll be your chaperone and remind you to leave room for Jesus when he gets too fresh. Are you really going to wait a week? Until he's forgotten that you even exist?"

"Well—"

"Do you want to make out with the coolest guy in school, or not?"

When she put it that way...

Sighing, Sarah stood up. Her vindicated friend clapped her hands together and looked up at the ceiling in gratitude. "Finally! She sees reason." Beaming, Jill grabbed Sarah's hand. "Come on, babe, I'll coach you through the call..."

A few minutes later they were giggling on the line like a couple of middle-schoolers, Jill bent over the phone that Sarah held so both could listen. When, a few rings in, Jack at last picked up, Sarah had to stifle a gasp. She stared fearfully into Jill's grinning face, mute for the first few seconds.

"Hello?"

Jack's voice! Sarah's diaphragm did flips. She would have forgotten to repeat the word back to him if not for Jill helpfully mouthing it at her.

"Uh—hello! Hi! Jack, it's, uh—it's Sarah. From the mall?"

"Sarah...oh! Oh, Sarah, hey. What's up?"

"Oh, you know...totally loving this chance to spend Saturday night inside, babysitting somebody else's kid. How's the album?"

"Man, totally righteous. Thanks again! That was sure cool of you. Hardly anybody else even knew it was my birthday."

"It was no biggie...um, hey"—Jill had been miming drinking liquor out of a bottle in the background of the call and, with this prompt, Sarah managed to get back on track—"so, what are you up to tonight?"

"Psht, nothing. It's this stupid curfew because of the sanitarium break-out. There's nothing going on this weekend and nothing to do but drive around and tip cattle and whatever."

Hey, charming. "Hah," said Sarah, her tone somewhat weaker at Jill's eyeroll for the athlete's boyish pastimes. "Yeah, well, I know that feeling..."

"Yeah—hey, but—you don't know anything going on tonight, do you? I'm dying to do *something*. If you knew where to get a beer I'd owe you for life."

While Jill theatrically mouthed the words, "Oh. My. God," Sarah grinned a little crookedly. She glanced toward the ceiling, the upstairs den beyond, the liquor cabinet waiting within it. "Totally, I do! Like, you could come over here—there's a whole bar."

"Whoa, really? All right, cool. Where are you?"

She gave him the address and he said, "Cool, right on—I think I can walk there. Isn't that off Main or whatever?" After Sarah had given him some directions, he said with morbid enthusiasm, "Wait, hold on! I know the place you're talking about now—isn't that—"

Sarah shot Jill an annoyed look, as though it were her fault. "Yeah, it's the Burr house. Does everybody know this but me? Would have been super freaking cool if the Johnsons had said something about it..."

"They probably didn't want to scare you off."

"No kidding...well, my friend Jill is here, too, so come any time. I think Billy's about to have his bedtime—"

"But I'm not tired," protested the eavesdropping child from where he was hidden around the kitchen doorway. Jill sucked a tooth while Sarah glanced sharply in the direction of the kid's voice.

"—so we can just relax and have a good night for the hour or two before his parents are back from the Bistro."

"Sounds like a plan...see you there, Sarah."

With stupid butterflies whizzing around her stomach at the sound of her name on Jack's lips, Sarah hung up the phone. She let her dorky grin drop only when she turned around and quite literally rolled up her sleeves.

"All right," Sarah said, briskly clapping her hands. "I think we've had enough horror movies...let's get this kid to bed and finally start the night!"

9.

IN FRONT of the Hugo residence, Chip Winston wrapped his report.

"Citizens are urged to stay in their homes until this is confirmed or denied, and until more facts come to light about the killer and his—or her—intentions. Reporting live from the scene, I'm Chip Winston, PCB Channel 5 News."

"....And we're good," said the cameraman with a half-assed wave.

Chip lowered his microphone with a sigh, not wasting a second before he began digging for his cigarette case.

"Thank God," the reporter said, extending the case to his coworker. The cameraman waved his hand. "You quitting?"

"Sure am. Had my last one two days ago."

"Good for you...this shit's going to be the death of me." Cigarette hanging from his mouth, Chip ducked his head over the lighter and then glanced back at the Hugo place. "What a creepy building this is. Like it was always waiting to be a murder house."

The camera guy laughed uneasily. "No kidding! I hate those upstairs windows. They look like eyes. Let me just deal with the footage in the production truck...could I ask you to wait outside for a minute? If I have to smell the smoke, I'm going to ask you for one. I just know it."

"Yeah, sure, whatever..." Waving him away, Chip puffed on his Camel and turned to study the façade of the building.

The Hugo residence loomed toward the starless October sky, seeming infinitely taller than it did on any ordinary day. Chip knew its height because he drove past it frequently when visiting his mother-in-law with his wife. She didn't live too far from here...it gave him the creeps to think how close this murderer had come to invading her *home instead of the Hugos'.*

Christ! When Chip got home, he was going to have to give her a call and check up on her. Didn't really like the lady, but didn't want her dead, either.

Footsteps scraped across the sidewalk. Chip didn't bother turning around to speak to his coworker, saying only, "Change your mind that fast, huh? Well, I hate to be the one to foster your bad habits—no, I'm not going to enable you in a moment of weakness.

Don't even ask."

The footsteps, which had paused for the duration of Chip's discouragement, now trailed back toward the van. A door opened.

His voice muffled from the back of the vehicle where he still dealt with the footage, the cameraman shouted in surprise as the van started. "Hey, what—"

At last Chip whipped around. He wouldn't understand how close to sudden death he came: not until a moment later. For now he only saw one thing.

A guy stealing the production van, Chip's cameraman still in the back.

"Hey! Hey, you son-of-a-bitch, stop!"

Throwing his cigarette away, the reporter dashed in front of the van, waved his arms, and threw himself atop the hood before the driver could get it into gear well enough to peel off. Chip banged on the windshield, squinting through, shouting again, "Stop—"

Until the face clicked in his mind.

No! Oh, no.

Stomach dropping beneath his feet, Chip leapt off the van and backed away with his hands in the air. "Take it," the reporter urged the man he recognized as the escaped killer holding the town hostage. "Go ahead, go on, take it."

If Burr listened to a word Chip had to say—if he was even aware of Chip's existence—he gave no indication. With the ignition roaring away, the startled cameraman burst out of the van. The doors swung shut behind him a second before Burr got the vehicle lurching into motion and he was mid-sentence, shouting, "What the hell's going on? I thought we were going to—what?"

He had been prepared to rant at Chip through the driver's side window. The cameraman instead found the reporter standing on the sidewalk, helplessness draining his features. Following his gaze to the side mirror, the cameraman glimpsed the face of Neoklaus Burr.

The van sped off.

From the look of shock on the cameraman's features, he recognized Burr a few seconds faster than had Chip. "Was that—"

"Yeah," said Chip, grimly, watching the van careen around the corner. "Yeah, it sure was."

The reporter looked down at the case of cigarettes in his hand and shuddered before looking around himself. "Uh…well, shit. What do we do now?"

"'What do we do now?' What we do now is you give me a fucking cigarette, Chip. Forget quitting! I'm going to smoke for the rest of my life."

That was looking very likely. Yes, very likely indeed. With trembling hands, Chip went back on his previous decision to support his friend's new and healthier lifestyle.

While they smoked, the cameraman demanded details that the reporter, perhaps ironically, wasn't able to offer. What had Burr sounded like? He hadn't said anything. What had he been carrying, if anything? The reporter hadn't turned around in time to see.

What did Chip think Burr was going to do with the van?

"Hell, I don't know. He was *going* somewhere, I guess."

"Well sure, yeah. But where was he going?"

Chip spread his hands. "I'm a reporter, not a psychic. I couldn't begin to guess. Hell! The guy really *must* be crazy. I mean, why go into the heart of town? You spend twenty-two years locked up in the loony bin, you bust out—don't you run away? Away from civilization, from cops? Don't you go anywhere else but the town that's on the lookout for you?"

"I don't know," suggested the cameraman. "Seems to me like he'd have a lot of rage. I would, at least. Wouldn't you?"

"Sure, but I wouldn't be killing anybody over it."

"Then I guess that's why you're not in the loony bin, huh, Chip?"

With a light laugh and a shake of his head, Chip agreed, "I guess," and exhaled a column of smoke through his nostrils.

Sniffing against the sting, smoothing his tie with his free hand, Chip stared at the looming Hugo house, its windows and glass paneled front doors dark. The façade had the effect of a face in the middle of a terrible scream.

Why was the human imagination so vivid? Chip

shook his anxiety off and tapped ash from his cigarette before turning to ask his colleague, "So what the hell are we going to do now?"

The cameraman wasn't listening, though. He had paused in the middle of his first cigarette in two days to frown.

Chip began to ask, "What is it?"

His colleague lifted his free hand. "Listen," the cameraman urged Chip softly.

A vehicle in the distance. A van?

"The production truck," said the cameraman seconds before the Channel 5 truck careened around the block to blaze down the street.

Chip barely had time to realize that Burr had driven around the block for the specific purpose of returning to kill them. The cameraman, crying out, instinctively shoved the reporter away from the edge of the sidewalk.

While Chip careened into the yard of the deceased Hugo family, the cameraman made the fatal mistake of trying to run across the street. Perhaps he hoped to split Burr's attention.

All this did was focus it.

The killer didn't even need to mount the sidewalk to hit the cameraman dead in the center of the van's bumper.

The wind was knocked out of him in a terrible groan and a series of snaps. Whether these were the sounds of breaking bones or of spidering windshield glass, Chip couldn't tell. He certainly wasn't going to stick around to look.

The van rumbled like a beast pawing the earth before its next charge. Chip scrambled upright, threw off his coat and sprinted around the side of the Hugo house without looking back.

The trouble was that Chip, like most reporters, was a somewhat doughy older man. He hadn't gotten fat with his middle years, but he wasn't in good shape, either. Certainly not good enough to flee a killer like Burr. And when you factored in the cigarette smoking? Forget it.

With Chip's arms pumping at a rapid clip, the panting started right away and only worsened by the step. His heart hammered in his chest. Jesus, he had heart problems! He was on medication. He could have dropped dead from the stress before Burr even set hands on him.

Somehow, gasping old Chip managed to scramble over the fence of the Hugo's back yard. He wondered for a few seconds if staying there wasn't the right thing to do, but the terror drove him on. The terror told him that if Burr didn't see Chip emerge, the solution to where he had gone would be obvious.

Breathless, slower all the time between his fatigue and inflamed smoker's lungs, Chip paused only briefly at the Hugos' fence before he forced himself to scale it.

He was not a climber, and the fence was a high privacy fence at nine feet, but desperation drove even unhealthy men to great feats of stamina.

Soon Chip was at the top. He covered his head in his arms before diving down to roll through the neighbors' yard, swearing only softly as he hit the ground.

Disoriented, sore, Chip scrambled up to see where he'd landed.

Ah! A family home! A family home with lights on and a television glowing bright blue inside.

Chip heard a laugh track. He heard comfort. His heart soared as he looked at the ranch-style house.

Here he could get help. Here—

Here a rottweiler snarled to have its territory invaded.

Its foaming jaws snapping at Chip's heels, the devoted dog chased the screaming reporter along the fence, through the gate, and out to the front lawn.

Evidently left to roam the yard unsupervised in the nighttime, the mongrel pursued this interloper to the edge of the grass and the sidewalk beyond, but there it stood and moved no farther.

"You stupid fucking mutt," shouted Chip, rolling upright, dusting himself off, checking his ass for injuries. When he looked back at the growling animal, he noticed the dog's shock collar. The reporter grinned.

"Ah, I get it now! Can't leave your yard, can you? Well screw you, pooch. I'll find help elsewhere, and your family will miss their chance to be the heroes who saved Chip Winston."

While the dog snarled in an effort to scare him off, Chip laughed. "You're mad, huh? What a stupid dog you are. Too bad your family never bothered to train you."

Chip turned away and laughed. The dog barked all the more wildly while the reporter limped his way to the next house on the block.

The dog's barking was such a constant and vicious refrain that by the time Chip heard the sound of the production truck, it was already barreling down the block right for him.

Its headlights surged past him, drawing his own shadow from relief until its head spilled up into the darkness with which it was conjoined. When Burr left the body behind, Chip's skull had been splattered open across the sidewalk just like that shadow.

No dog would have been able to resist this once-in-a-lifetime opportunity. The rottweiler leapt through its invisible barrier, absorbed the punishing zap to its neck, and hurried over to eat the dead man's face.

Inside the house, its family guffawed along with a final burst of canned laugh track that signaled the end of their sitcom. They turned to another station as soon as the news came on.

10.

PUTTING BILLY to bed took an impressive twenty minutes once the reluctant boy had brushed his teeth, mostly because he insisted the girls tell him a story. Jill had been kind enough to whip up one that wasn't too scary. The kid had even dozed off a little by the end—though he demanded, as they were creeping out, "Leave the door cracked, please...I want the hall light."

So they couldn't be too loud...but at least Billy was out of the way for now. In the den, the girls chatted about what music to play from the Johnson's somewhat lacking collection. "This old stuff sucks," Jill decided unilaterally. "Let's just watch TV instead."

Not the best idea. *Night of the Living Dead* had reached its grim conclusion already. Its Romero-approved sequel, *Dawn of the Dead,* was now being played—with plentiful commercials to take advantage of the movie's relative newness. Jill rolled her eyes to recognize it after a few frames. "For real? No, thanks... back off, zombies, Sarah's scared."

"Shut up, bitch."

"Bite me, loser." Jill laughed while changing stations, asking seconds before the newscaster with his tweed suit and trench coat fizzled into relief across the screen, "Hey, do they have any nosh? Like, popcorn? I'm mega starved—"

"—dead several hours prior to police response."

Jill fell quiet. The young women exchanged a glance before focusing together on the grim expression of a local reporter whose face they'd both seen many times.

Chip Winston stood in front of a nice suburban home—one of the newer ones in a development Sarah recognized with a chill as being not so very far from her own home. The front lawn had been cordoned off with yellow police tape that twisted in the October wind.

While viewers absorbed the scene, the reporter continued, "It is currently suspected that the Hugo's killer is the same escaped mental patient responsible for the riot at Monroe State Hospital on Friday night."

"Hugo." Jill looked at Sarah. "Isn't Mr. Hugo, like, a music teacher or something? Katrina Bixby has class with him..."

Sarah couldn't reply. She was too focused on the

broadcast to think of anything to say.

The reporter continued grimly, "Citizens are urged to stay in their homes until this is confirmed or denied, and until more facts come to light about the killer and his—or her—intentions."

The camera cut back to the well-Aquanetted female reporter who sat behind the desk at the Channel 5 station. She stared blankly for several seconds before receiving her cue.

"That was Chip Winston on the scene of an ongoing murder investigation. Our hearts go out to the friends and families of the Hugos, and of Vernon Brown, whose body, we are learning, was found mere moments ago. He is another suspected homicide victim police are tentatively linking to the Burr escape.

"For those just tuning in, the Monroe County Sheriff's Department has issued the warning to stay inside. Citizens are urged to avoid answering the door for any unexpected visitors until further notice. We'll bring you more information as the situation develops: stay tuned for emergency updates."

"No, bitch, that's okay." Jill flipped to the next station with a look of absolute derision. "Ugh! There's literally nothing on. Whatever. Zombies it is, I guess... we'll just turn it down to keep from waking you-know-who. Dude, are you okay?" Jill had glanced over at Sarah to read her mood and clearly didn't like what she found. "You look super pale."

"Yeah, yeah, of course. I'm fine. Just—you don't

really think it was Burr who killed those people, do you?"

"Well, like...it would be way freakier if he didn't."

"For sure," agreed Sarah after thinking about it for a second. "I guess I'd rather there be, one escaped killer than, like, one escaped killer and one secret killer."

"Ugh...now you're creeping *me* out. Fuck this! We're being stupid, we should be partying! You got Jack to come over! Aren't you, like, totally excited?"

"Totally," agreed Sarah as her friend went on with great enthusiasm for things Sarah just couldn't make herself care about.

Sarah tried to relax. The truth though was that she was so wound up by all this talk of Burr and his killings and his sanitarium escape—how could she think of anything else? How could she think of anything but the phone call?

How could she think of anything but the mask?

"You're doing it again," said Jill in an openly hostile tone.

Sarah tuned back into the conversation, lifting her face from the hand where it had come to rest. Jill waved her rum and coke with a belligerent air. "You're *such* a freaking space cadet! I start talking about anything and you just, like, drift right off. I'm surprised you didn't fall asleep along with Billy just now!"

"Sorry. I'm just distracted... Can I be honest with you?" Sheepishly glancing into her drink and then back up to Jill, Sarah confessed, "I guess I am actually kind of freaked."

"Oh, whatever. Nothing bad is going to happen...it was just a weird coincidence that this turned out to be the Burr house. Sorry I brought it up."

Sarah was not to be so easily consoled. "But, like—I don't know. When I was looking for the liquor cabinet key earlier, there was like...ugh, this weird, creepy crawlspace I found. It had this knife all covered in rust, and, like...this *mask,* I don't know. You don't think—like, that's not something related to Burr, is it?"

At last interested, Jill lowered her drink. "Oh shit, dude! Maybe. What kind of knife? Where's this crawlspace?"

Sarah led her to the moved bookshelf, explaining, "I don't think anybody's even been in it since the Johnsons moved in, or maybe before...it's a super small door. I don't think anybody can even really fit in there."

"Dude, that's way small. You're so petite! What a bitch. I'm so jealous of you."

Laughing mildly, Sarah admitted, "Being small has its benefits...anyway, come here, borrow this." She handed her friend the pocket flashlight and tugged open the protesting little door while saying, "If you kind of stick your head in, you might be able to at least see the mask."

"Hold on...there aren't spiders in there, are there?"

"Probably, like, a whole freaking colony of brown

recluses."

"Shut *up*..." Shoving Sarah aside, Jill rolled her eyes and knelt while muttering, "Trying to freak me out, get bent...okay, so where's this—ah!"

Jill's whole body jolted so sharply upon noticing the freaky mask that she slammed her head up into the small doorway. "Shit! Ah, ow—"

Rubbing the top of her skull, Jill admitted, "Damn, okay, you're right. That's super spooky."

"Right? Can you see the knife, too?"

"I don't know...where is it?"

"It's like, way back behind a wood beam back there, kind of leaning against the wall—"

"Oh! Woah! There it is. Way to see, eagle eye...gosh, no wonder they never found the murder weapon."

Sarah's heart skipped a beat at that. Like, really skipped a beat. She hadn't known that wasn't just a clichéd metaphor and found herself leaning against the wall. "You really think that's the murder weapon?"

"Well, like, the cops didn't find one sticking out of a body or dropped on the floor or whatever, so I think they just assumed it was one of the kitchen knifes in the sink. That he, like, cleaned it or something. Cops are so fucking lazy..."

"Don't repeat that when Jack is over here...I think he said his uncle is a cop."

"Lame! You sure do like meat-heads, huh, biker bitch?"

"I'm not a biker bitch yet! You can't call me that

until I actually have a motorcycle. Anyway…you're not just messing with me, are you?"

"I sort of wish I were, because it's legit pretty freaky to think this might be a murder weapon. But, I mean, look at it! Doesn't that stuff look like blood to you?"

Paled, Sarah accepted the flashlight back once her friend's upper half wiggled out of the cramped opening. Bending and squeezing first her arm, then her head and shoulders through the hole, Sarah illuminated the blade. The whole time she tried, for whatever paranoid or superstitious reason, to avoid shining her light on or even looking at the face of the mask.

Looking at the knife again, Jill was right. That wasn't rust—at least, not all of it. Something had coated the surface of the blade, discoloring it before corroding it, and the overall effect was gnarly to say the least. If a knife could be diseased, this one was.

"This is so warped," said Sarah, more to herself than to Jill.

"Right? Way to go, Sarah! Even I've got the creeps now…"

"Sorry! How do you think I feel? I'm the one who's been babysitting at a murder house without realizing it all this time. With a murder weapon still in the *walls,* no less!"

"Jeez, well—yeah, that sucks. Ugh, I don't know." Fidgeting from foot to foot, Jill at last suggested, "Let's throw that stuff out. The Johnsons don't want it in their house, for sure."

"Don't you think we should give it to the cops or something?"

"For a solved case that's, like, two decades old? Whatever! No way. They don't care, we don't care— let's throw that stuff out."

Sarah frowned at the knife. The hollow grimace of the clown face waited in her periphery, staring through her soul as she mustered a response.

"I don't want to touch it," Sarah reluctantly confessed, glancing over her shoulder toward the doorway and making accidental eye contact with the empty holes of the mask. Her skin crawled and she averted her gaze as quickly as she could.

"You baby! Well *I* can't get it out of that crawlspace, and Jack's going to be too big, for sure. You want Billy to be fooling around and find it someday? He'll have freaking nightmares for life!"

"Ugh, you're right...whatever! This is ultra morbid."

"Right? Hold on. Let me get you, like, a towel or something so you don't have to actually put your hands on it—"

Jill stepped away before Sarah could wiggle out to join her. Then, there she was, then.

Alone, upper half inside the crawlspace, the mask staring her down amid the silence of its hateful pagliacco laugh.

You know what? This was stupid. She was being

stupid. Jill was absolutely right: Sarah was being ridiculous. There was no proof this had anything to do with Burr in the first place.

So, the house had once been his. So, people had died there. So, that night had been horrific. Okay, fine.

Twenty years had passed since that crime, though. The house had exchanged hands more than once, based on Billy's age and some things Jill and the Johnsons both had said. Surely this stuff could have found its way into the crawlspace since then.

Surely all this didn't mean anything.

Sarah forced herself to not just illuminate the mask, but to stare into it. Its empty eyes stared back, the wooden beam to which it was stuck by an exposed nail lending its gaze a kind of strange texture—a kind of shape to its otherwise absent orbs. She frowned.

What was this mask doing here? The knife, she could almost understand. She could see how a killer with no real concern about being caught might just toss his murder weapon anywhere, not caring if it was found or not. But this mask?

This mask was something else. Somehow, it bothered her far more. Maybe because it was a child's mask.

Or maybe because, as Jill approached, Sarah noticed a chunk of human hair was stuck to the nail. A little piece of scalp, tangled in the decayed elastic of the brittle plastic mask.

"Here," Jill said, interrupting Sarah's thoughts by

brusquely thrusting a pair of yellow dish gloves down at her friend. "I grabbed a garbage bag, too. Just get that junk out and toss it in here."

With great relief, Sarah did as her friend advised. She yanked the gloves onto her hands and, delicately, grimacing the whole time, extended an arm while she squeezed herself farther into the crawlspace.

Oh, man...was she even going to be able to reach it? This space was so small. Maybe they could just get the mask out and enlist Billy to get the knife. Tell him it's—

Ah! Phew—her fingertip barely brushed the blade, tickling its rusted edge and coaxing it toward her. It listed like a falling tree in her direction.

She managed to catch the handle with a cry of victory. Pleased, Sarah squeezed out from the crawlspace and brandished the knife in the light.

Somehow, it was even worse out in the open. Sarah and Jill both stared down at a blade coated almost to the handle with dried red fluid that had, in most places, decayed to jagged rust.

"I feel like I need a tetanus shot just after *looking* at this thing," marveled Jill grimly, remembering at the last second to actually open the garbage bag she clutched to her chest. "That's sick, dude. I'm totally going to hurl! Can you believe that thing was used to kill a kid?"

"I don't even want to think about it," said Sarah. She turned away and reached again into the crawlspace, this time without looking. Her hand groped blindly around the wood beam until it brushed the mask.

After feeling around to the back, she tugged the elastic loop up over the nail and freed it from its long confinement.

"There," said Sarah with pleasure, tossing the mask into the garbage bag without even looking at it. Jill shut the bag with a pleased smile and didn't bother tying it, what with how little garbage it contained.

Sarah unpeeled the yellow rubber from her hands. "Are these gloves disposable?"

"They are now," said Jill, plucking the things from Sarah's hands and adding them to the bag with a grin. While Sarah rolled her eyes, Jill said, "Oh, whatever, like they're going to miss dish gloves...you can buy them new ones when they cough up your payment from last time. Come on! Let's get this shit thrown out and get back to partying. No wonder our vibe was so bogus!"

Yeah, well...Sarah couldn't help but feel there were plenty of other reasons for the bogus vibe, but she couldn't deny that the thought of getting a twenty-year-old murder weapon out of the house made her feel a little bit better.

At Jill's suggestion, Sarah agreed to throw it out in the garbage cans alongside the house rather than in the kitchen garbage.

"You have to come with me, though," protested Sarah. Jill didn't even roll her eyes, though she didn't look happy.

"Sure," said Jill, glancing at the window. "It's mega dark out there already, huh."

The magic of October. Both far tenser than they would have been on any normal night but neither willing to admit it, Sarah and Jill opened the front door. They stepped together into the darkness.

The wind whipped up Sarah's ponytail while Jill's thoroughly sprayed hairdo failed to budge.

Sarah peered down the length of the house's garage and to the corner near the garbage cans.

Her friend sucked a tooth. "Where's that freaking flashlight?"

Good idea. Sarah turned it on, then scoffed to find how little the beam did when it had so much space to work in. "Wow," said Jill dryly, "okay. That's somehow almost worse. Like a—"

"Don't say—"

"—horror movie or something." As Sarah rolled her eyes and shoved past her friend to climb down from the porch's side stairs, Jill hurried behind her. "At least it'll keep us from, like, tripping over something."

"Do you have to cling to me like that, Jill?"

"I'm just supporting you! I don't want you to be scared."

"This reminds me of that haunted house we did last October...now that I think about it, you were, like, squeezing off my freaking hand! Maybe it's you who's the scaredy-cat, bitch."

Almost home-free—Sarah lifted the lid of the trash can at the garage's corner while her friend gasped indignantly.

"Sarah, you whore! I'm not *scared.* You're the one who's scared. Like I said, I just want you to know that I'm—"

As the figure leapt from the corner of the garage, Sarah and Jill both screamed.

11.

THE BLOOD-SPLATTERED production van crawled the town's streets at a slow pace, its headlights off. Its driver was oriented well enough without them, and though such a thing would have attracted the attention of police, low visibility kept random citizens from noticing the vehicle by means of its lights or the unfortunate rumble it produced at higher speeds.

Leisure could be afforded. If the police resources had been stretched thin before, they were at a breaking point now. The number of crime scenes left along Burr's spree meant it was only a matter of time before additional resources were called in.

Maybe the FBI—at this rate, the national guard. The poor town just wasn't psychologically equipped for a thing like that. But had it been equipped for anything that happened that night? Certainly not. The cops hadn't been, at least, and their uncertainty combined with their thin resources to give Burr a very low sense of urgency.

And, anyway...such a homecoming was to be savored. It had been so long. Twenty years. Would the house still be the same? The yard? The crawlspaces?

During the trial, the prosecution hadn't been able to provide a definitive murder weapon. Amazing they hadn't been willing to tear the wall down and investigate the crawlspace. Burr was more than willing to gut the structure to get to the one weapon that mattered to him.

The night had been a matter of so much improvisation. Improvised tool after improvised tool had claimed one life at a time and been thrown away. Even that first gun taken off of the security guard: that had been empty by the time Burr finished with the jogger.

All he really wanted was his home—his true, bloody home. Burr's only tangible desire was the knife that had felt like home in his hand while he plunged it again and again into the unprepared body of his wife.

If he could have enjoyed one minute of his life over again, that one would have been the one. The knife couldn't literally bring him back in time, but it could certainly help him relive his happiest moment.

Only once on his way through the semi-familiar town did Burr narrowly avoid a police cruiser. This one must have been held up at a separate crime, something unrelated to Burr. It now rushed through the streets with its lights flashing and its siren blaring loud through the paralyzed neighborhoods. Might have been on the way to the scene of the reporter's death.

If it was, its driver wasn't the most attentive cop on the force. With such advance notice, the killer had ample time to pull the van to the side of the dark street down which it crawled.

Two seconds later, the screeching cruiser blazed past. It whipped right by the blood-splattered news van that had parked nose-to-tail with a nearby family sedan.

So far as any onlooker could have told, the cop didn't even turn his head toward the Channel 5 logo emblazoned clearly on the stolen vehicle's side.

Burr waited in the dark, temporarily parked car until the cop was out of sight and had been given a good thirty seconds to drive down the street he'd taken. Then, with a miserable grumble, the production van restarted beneath its thief's hand and reluctantly eased into the road again.

Wasn't far now. These corners, these mailboxes—these houses. Even with an occasional alteration here or there, Burr could have driven the route in his sleep. He frequently dreamed of it. He didn't remember much else about his dreams.

Finally, after turning down his old street, Burr found it completely unchanged. The neighborhood had been stopped in time. The crime had rippled out:

as death froze the body in motion, the murders in the Burr household had stopped the development of the street. Nothing was modern about these houses, these yards. Everything was sill.

Everything except a bit of motion. Animal? No. Well—yes, and no.

A young man in a letter jacket walking down the sidewalk.

The production van slowed to an all the more agonizing crawl as Burr stalked along the sidewalk a few more feet.

Then, unexpectedly, the boy stopped in front of the same house that had captured the killer's attention from the distant corner. His house. Burr's house. The boy walked up the driveway to the Burr house.

The production van picked up its pace. Neoklaus cruised by without looking too long at the boy; the home; the two girls who emerged from the front door and caused the boy, after a second of delay, to duck around the corner of the garage.

All right.

Maybe he did look too long.

At the opposite end of the block, Neoklaus parked the bloody van with its hood pressed against an oleander bush to obscure the gore smeared across the bumper. Turned out Chip wore a toupee, apparently. This cluster of blood and false hair disentangled itself at the touch of the oleanders and dropped to the street while the van shut off.

Burr paused only to search the glove box for another improvisational device. He found a passable solution almost immediately. The screwdriver palmed in his hand, Burr left the truck and made his way down the unlit suburban street.

Cars, trees, shrubs, fences; everything provided him camouflage as he neared the house from which a pair of shrieks rose before he had even completed his approach.

Then, his keen senses caught it. Just a single snippet of the children's chatter, but a most welcome one. Burr caught this valuable information as he crouched behind the white car parked along the house's sidewalk, where he was invisible in the thick darkness of the autumn night.

The teenagers stood with their heads bent over a bag. "Wowee," said the boy, "holy cow—is this for real? Like, is this straight up the knife he used to kill his family?"

That, and certain parts of the following conversation, were extremely interesting to him. Sheltered behind that white muscle car, Burr bowed his head and listened carefully.

The minute they were inside, he popped the hood of the car with his screwdriver and got right to work.

12.

SARAH'S SCREAM was so loud that she couldn't hear Jack's laughter until long after Jill's matching shriek reached a conclusion.

As Sarah fell back a step with her hand on her chest, Jill recognized him and burst into absolute fury.

"You fuckin' *twerp!* You stupid *punk!* Jumping out at us like that when there's a killer on the loose—"

"You should have seen your *faces!* Holy shit! *Ha-ha-ha—*"

"Whatever, loser! That's super not funny." Sarah now had frame of mind enough to join in on the remonstration, though she bore the hint of a grin she struggled to hide while telling Jack off. "We could have seriously hurt you. What if we had punched you, or something?"

Jill's hands had settled on her hips. "Yeah—or Sarah could have hit you with the garbage bag and you could have been stabbed by a twenty-year-old murder weapon. Like, enjoy your lockjaw, shit-for-brains!"

Scoffing, Sarah agreed and asked, "What are you doing lurking around the garage, anyway?"

"Aw, come on—I was just fooling around." Still laughing, Jack straightened his letter jacket and said, "I was just about to come up the porch when I heard you two coming out the door. Guess I picked the right spot to hide...it was perfect!"

"Total jerk," said Jill, shoving him in the arm, her expression soured against the effort it took her to avoid being amused.

"I guess it was sort of funny," admitted Sarah, dumping the bag into the open can until Jack bent his head.

Peering at the bag, the boy asked, "So what are you talking about, murder weapon? I just saw a news truck drive by—is this about the Burr thing?"

Jill quickly forgot her anger in the face of lurid excitement. "Okay, check it out: Sarah found this in a crawlspace or whatever—give me that flashlight, Sarah—"

With Jill manning the beam, Sarah opened the garbage bag and all three bent their heads over to see. The athlete boggled at the contents. "Wowee, holy cow—is this for real? Like, is this straight up the knife he used to kill his family?"

Jill laughed snidely. "Well, dude, I don't think it's

Clamato on that old-ass knife we found in a wall."

"Far out...what's that freaky mask doing in there?"

"No idea. Don't even really super want to know." Sarah shut the bag and dumped it once and for all in the garbage can. What a triumph it was to slam that lid down! "There—good riddance."

Jill gave the garbage can the finger. "Yeah! Fuck you, bad vibes! Get out of here. Let's party!" She lifted her hand for an enthusiastic high-five that Jack was quick to return.

"Wooh! Party! All right, let's get some brewskis going."

The trio laughed all the way up the porch stairs, cares forgotten, and continued laughing until Sarah tried the front doorknob.

"Oh," she whispered sharply, "shit!"

"Sarah." Jill stared at her, wide-eyed. "Don't even tell me."

Jack leaned around them both. "What's the problem?"

"Shit," repeated Sarah, this time with more vigor. Jill slapped herself in the forehead and stomped her foot like a child.

"It's freaking *locked?* You *locked us out?* Way to go, Major Tom! This bitch." Sighing and shaking her head at Jack, Jill said, "Sarah's always off in outer space, dude...it's amazing to me that she wants to buy a motorcycle. You need, like, reflexes and attention and shit."

"Shut up, you bitch." While laughing, Sarah nonetheless punched Jill in the arm.

Jack laughed along. "Do you ride a bike, too, Jill?"

"Nah, that's my car over there. I'm going to sound like a freaking grandma, but I hate bikes. Like, 'buy your son a motorcycle for his last birthday,' you know?"

"Psht, whatever. Guess Sarah's cooler than you—"

"As if!"

Normally Sarah would have been flattered by Jack bringing her up in any brand of flirtatious teasing, but she was a little distracted. Yeah, the door was locked for sure, and no happy key waited under the mat.

She had only one unfortunate choice. Sighing, Sarah began to knock vigorously at the front door. "Billy," she called while Jill groaned in displeasure.

"No! We just got that little shit to sleep."

"He's not a little shit, he's a nice kid. He was just in a bad mood tonight because his parents suck and think that letting him do whatever he wants makes up for not giving him enough attent— Billy!"

The door opened. All three teenagers beamed at the kid, sleep-ruffled and blinking as he stood on the threshold.

In a drowsy voice, the half-asleep boy asked, "How come you woke me up?"

Sarah laughed awkwardly. "Sorry, little dude. We got stuck outside while putting away the garbage."

"Oh," said the boy while watching the older people

trail past. "Hey, who's that?"

"Oh! Uh! This is my friend, Jack." Man! One of the reasons Sarah called Jack at all was because the kid was finally in bed. That way she wouldn't have to worry about him telling his parents that his babysitter had a boyfriend over. Now, though—ugh.

The Johnsons were totally going to use this as an excuse to stiff her. She could feel it coming.

Well...might as well party.

The curious boy, more awake by the second, continued probing. "How come he's here?"

"Because now *I'm* freaked out," Jill answered helpfully. "Talking with you about zombies got me way scared, man! We had to call a boy to keep us from getting spooked."

"My mom never gets scared of anything," Billy curtly informed them as if to prove his mother's superiority to all other females in existence.

Laughing, Sarah shepherded the boy in the direction of the staircase. "Well, your mom's sure cool! You guys go ahead and hang out down here for a minute, okay? I'll just put Billy back to bed...back in five." Sarah took him by the hand. "Come on, little bro."

"Good night," the boy called while Sarah guided him back upstairs. "Sorry my movie scared you, Sarah."

"That's okay, buddy." With a fond chuckle for the genuinely cute kid, Sarah patted his head and led him to his room near the top of the stairs. "Let's just get you back to sleep. Hopefully you'll have better dreams than I will tonight, huh?"

"Oh, I'm not scared of anything except the bogeyman."

"Well, at least the bogeyman isn't real, so you don't have to be afraid of that."

"Really? My grandma always said that if I didn't go to sleep when she told me to, the bogeyman would come and get me."

"Ah, adults tell kids all kinds of lame lies about stuff like that. I don't like to mess around. I just say, 'Go to bed.' And on that note...go to bed!"

Billy laughed despite himself, asking, "Will you tuck me in?"

"Sure! Let's get cozy. Here you go."

"And will you tell me a story?"

Sarah rolled her eyes, trying not to smile too much as she smoothed the blankets over his shoulder. "You already got a story tonight, buddy."

"But *another story.*"

"Nice try, but that's not how it works. One official bedtime, one official bedtime story...I can't help that you're breaking curfew right now. Trying to bust out of prison."

Billy sat back up right away. His eyes were wild with the same enthusiasm that leaked into his voice. "Like that crazy guy? Like on the news? The killer they were talking about?"

"Hey! Were you listening to that news broadcast

from up here?" At the boy's sheepish grin, Sarah rolled her eyes savagely. She was never going to hear the end of it if he had nightmares because of this. "No more eavesdropping! That's a bad habit."

"I was just curious! Is he really killing people?"

Sarah spread her hands helplessly. "I guess. You know about as much as I do."

"You don't think he'd come here, do you?"

"Oh, Billy—" She glanced toward the door and its golden strip of hall light, then patted his head one more time. "I wish you hadn't listened to that broadcast. You shouldn't scare yourself."

"I'm not scared," protested the boy instinctively, then glancing askance and admitting, "well, okay. Maybe I am a little scared…I wish Mom and Dad were home tonight."

"They'll be home soon, Billy. Until then, you've got me. Plus, it's nice to know my friends are here, too."

"Yeah." The boy nodded, willing to agree that he was mollified even if he didn't actually feel it. "It feels safer with more people in the house."

"That's right. If anybody tries to pull anything, they'll have all three of us to deal with."

The boy nodded at that. "Dad says when I'm older he'll teach me how to shoot. Then I'll be able to protect myself, and I won't have to worry. Until then, I'm glad you're here."

"I'm glad, too, Billy."

Yeah. You know, in a weird way, she really was.

Sure, Billy was kind of an unreasonable little punk, but so was every kid his age when you got right down to it. They were sensitive, kids, and had so many changes of temper from moment to moment. All those hormones still finding their feet had a way of really messing with their moods.

And, as far as kids went, Billy was among the better-tempered. Sarah had to remember that he was smart. Smart, and more than capable of picking up on the tension of adults around him. Even when they thought they hid their feelings, adults had ways of telegraphing everything to the children in their lives. Sarah therefore smiled confidently as she patted the kid's hand.

"You go to sleep now, okay?"

"Okay, Sarah. Good night."

"Good night Part II, Billy."

While the boy laughed, Sarah smiled, cracked the door, and practically skipped with joy on her way back down to party with her friends.

Hell yes! Thanks for going back to bed easily, Billy.

Truly grateful, Sarah hurried toward the sound of the television, braced for more zombies. Instead she entered the Johnson living room to find her friends glued to a news broadcast.

"—received another bulletin from police mere moments ago, once again urging citizens to stay indoors at all costs. Turn off your lights, ensure doors and windows are bolted, and if you have a gun, be prepared to use it in an emergency scenario: but by no means are civilians advised to engage with the suspect, or make any attempts at vigilantism."

Sarah's expression tensed as she sat with her friends. The reporter went on, her tone as grim as the atmosphere in the living room where the three teenagers sat. "Burr is considered extremely dangerous. Until he's caught, Monroe County Sheriff's deputies urge strict adherence to these guidelines."

"I wish Frank's Bistro had a radio," said Sarah to herself. "Or a television at their bar."

"Whatever." Snapping out of it and flipping the channel back to the zombie movie, Jill insisted, "They're just, like, exaggerating. The news always wants to keep butts in seats. I'm sure they've been just, like, beside themselves all day with the opportunity to drag out their reporting and get people super scared. Fear is how you control people. That's what my dad says."

Though not disagreeing, Sarah smiled a little and teased, "Your dad says that because he's a hippie."

"Whatever! He's not a hippie, he fought in Vietnam. He taught me how to shoot! Just because his hair is long now, you stuck-up bitch..."

"Stuck-up! I'm not the one who's suddenly all anti-motorcycle."

Plastic bracelets clinking on her wrists while she waved her drink, Jill scoffed. "I just don't want you to get killed, okay? Sheesh!"

Jack, glancing between them, laughed a little. "You two have a weird friendship."

"Oh, her?" Jill grinned at Sarah and insisted, "As if! Who would want to be friends with Sarah?"

"Yeah, nobody wants to hang out with Jill. What a bitch!" While the girls laughed, Sarah leaned down and hugged her friend around the shoulders. Jill patted her back.

Sarah, emboldened by the camaraderie, straightened up and said, "I'm gonna go grab a beer from the kitchen, I think I saw a couple in the back of the fridge earlier. You guys want one?"

"Hell yeah," said Jack, looking down at his nearly empty glass. "'Liquor before beer, you're in the clear.'"

"Get one for me, too, babe," Jill called while Sarah ducked out of the living room and down the dark hall to the kitchen.

And she was very nearly there when the crash rang out from the Johnson's back yard.

B.

SARAH WOULD have been so happy if she could have convinced herself she was hearing things. Yes, it would have been great! Great to live in oblivious bliss, in safety and comfort. Great to not suffer from the plague of paranoia.

But there were no two ways about it. There was no convincing herself she had imagined it. Sarah had heard a noise in the back yard. What was it, exactly?

She wasn't sure, but when she tried to play it back in her head—a kind of grinding followed by a metallic thump—it reminded her of the way the gate to her grandmother's garden sounded from inside the house.

Feeling the blood drain from her face, Sarah turned around and burst back into the living room.

Her friends looked up as she asked, "Did you guys

hear that?"

Jack lowered the rum and coke from his lips. "Hear what?"

"That crash. A noise like—like the side gate opening and slamming shut, or something."

"What? No way." Wrinkling her nose, Jill said, "Quit messing with us."

"No, for real. I'm not playing around. I heard something. Here, turn down the TV."

Upon hurrying to the remote, Sarah lowered the volume of the movie. She stared into the distance with unfocused eyes while waiting for any other out-of-place noise.

And she waited.

And she waited.

"You are so full of it," Jill declared, breaking Sarah's concentration and producing a scowl from her.

"I *swear*. I absolutely heard something."

"I guess I did kind of hear some thump or whatever," Jack admitted, glancing at the screen. "I thought it was just the movie, though."

Sarah looked between her friends, brow furrowed. "With everything going on, and Billy upstairs—I mean, we can't just *stand* here."

Aggressively unimpressed, Jill propped her cheek upon her free hand. She whined, "This is so lame! What do you want to do about it, Sarah? Because I think we should just ignore your imaginary noises. And instead of freaking out over nothing, maybe we should try, you know—having fun."

"You can't have fun when you're dead, Jill."

"Says the bitch saving up for a fucking motor-cycle...ugh! You can't seriously think we should *do* something about your noise."

"*We* shouldn't, you're right." While Jill looked at her dryly and waited for her to complete her thought, Sarah admitted, "I think we should call the cops. Better safe than sorry."

"What!" Glancing sidelong at the boy who, she had been recently informed, was related to at least one cop, Jill opted to keep her opinions relatively mild. "Are you kidding? We're sitting here with hard liquor in our hands and you want to get the cops at the door? They'll take one look at us, say we've had one too many, and freaking slap us on the wrists for wasting their time. I don't want to deal with it."

"Well," said Sarah, "we have to do something."

Jill sighed far more heavily this time. She looked at Sarah for a sustained length. Then, slowly, she turned her gaze toward Jack.

The quarterback had been staring as if lost in thought. Only when Sarah also looked at him, seeing the possibilities, did he snap out of it. Jack looked between the girls and, suddenly understanding the meaning of their stares, looked almost frightened.

"I mean..." He looked somewhat desperately over at Jill. "It was probably just a cat or something, right?"

Sarah tapped her foot in an emulation of her mother's most impatient habit. She forced herself to stop when she realized what she was doing, but she still pointed out, "Cats can't open doors, Jack."

"How do you know it was actually the sound of the fence opening? It could have just been, like, a raccoon leaping down or something. Claws scraping, or whatever."

"Please, Jack?" Clasping her hands, Sarah put on her best helpless expression and urged the boy, "It would mean so much to me. Really. I'm sure you guys are right and it's totally nothing...but it would settle my mind if you could just check. There's the kid to think about, you know?"

"Man..." Sighing, pondering the contents of his glass, Jack forced the rest of the burning liquid down his throat and grimaced. After shaking it off, he rose unsteadily to his feet. "Is there, like, a baseball bat or something around here?"

"I don't know—we don't really have time to look, do we? Look, just please stick your head out and see if there's somebody out there."

"All right," said Jack with a hefty sigh. "All right, I'll just check...scare your raccoon away..."

"Thank you." With a sigh of relief, Sarah led him toward the kitchen and its back door. "I really appreciate it. I know I'm being a total loser tonight, but—"

"Nah, I get it...it's responsible, or whatever." Jack shared a glance with the doleful bloodhounds arranged in the oil painting poised over the couch. His hangdog stare reflected the ones that came naturally to them. "Just—what if we *did* call the cops, though?"

"Oh my God." Jill stomped her foot and pointed at the light spilling down the hall from the kitchen. "Go out there and just get it over with! Come on. There's nothing there."

Smoothing the front of his letter jacket with a reflexive hand, Jack shuffled through the kitchen, sighed, opened the back door, then shut it behind him.

"You're going to feel like a total dweeb tomorrow morning," Jill warned Sarah as both girls hovered nervously on the edge of the kitchen. "And if all this opening and closing the back door disturbs that kid again, I'm going to be *super* freaking annoyed."

"It'll take Jack two minutes…I just need peace of mi—"

Jack's scream—almost a wail, of anguish as much as of agony—was so abrupt, so sharp, and so prolonged that the girls froze in place. The sound was impossibly horrible. They didn't even jump, or grab one another.

Instead of provoking normal fear, the scream seemed to have some other power. Some means by which it altered the teenagers' consciousnesses.

Yes, that was it. Sarah felt not a chill but a shift in her own internal body chemistry. Her awareness of every sound increased threefold. Only when the scream ended did she grip Jill's arm—and then, only to catch her eye and find her pale as Sarah was.

"What was that?"

Jill's desperate whisper made Sarah realize how terribly afraid they both were. All her friend's brava- do vanished. With it went Sarah's final traces of hope that she was just being paranoid.

"That—that was Jack. The door! We have to lock the door—call the police, Jill, quick—"

"Fuck," said Jill, rushing to the phone mounted on the kitchen wall while Sarah hurried to snap the lock shut. "Fuck, fuck—"

The screaming seemed to echo still in Sarah's ears. While adrenaline pumped through Sarah's limbs at the behest of her racing heart, Jill gasped and hit the phone hook a few rapid times. "Oh, man—the phone's dead, Sarah—"

"What? What do you mean?"

"I mean the phone's *dead,* bitch! What are you, deaf? Holy shit, holy shit—oh, my God!"

Total darkness enveloped the house.

"Holy shit," repeated Jill uselessly, now rushing over to grip Sarah's arm. "Oh, no! Oh, fuck! What are we going to do?"

"Okay," said Sarah. "Okay, let's stay calm—oh, shit, okay—"

Trying to steady the tremor of her hand, Sarah pulled the flashlight out of her pocket and illuminat- ed the corner of the Johnson's kitchen. As the beam flooded the sink of dirty dishes and then swept to- ward the hall, Sarah told her friend, "Billy said there was a fuse box in the garage—I don't know if it's going to do any good."

"The power is *out,* Sarah! It's clearly out. I don't think we have time to fuck around with fuse boxes! And what about Jack? Oh, holy shit, dude—oh, Sarah—"

"Just stay calm. Stay calm. He could be—he could have been surprised." Swallowing back her fear as best she could, Sarah put her hand on the knob. Reluctantly, she unlocked it, then opened the door to the back screen. "Or maybe he's just messing with us again."

"I don't know, dude…I don't know."

With a look of helpless horror at what they were about to do, Jill said, "Hold on." She leapt away from Sarah to collect a kitchen knife.

When Jill returned, it quivered in the light along with her hand. The girls took a deep breath together.

Sarah pushed open the screen.

Then, they were outside. Jill shut the door behind them and the two scanned the darkness of the yard, whisper-calling, "Jack? Jack? Are you there?"

Absolute silence was the only response. Sarah noticed with a further, altogether more awful chill that the houses of neighbors still glowed with electric comforts. The Johnsons' house was the only one with the power out.

"This is too warped," whispered Jill. She clung to Sarah with one hand, the other prepared to slash into the darkness at any moment.

The beam of Sarah's flashlight flooded across the yard. It shone across the edge of the padlocked shed, pulling it out from the rest of the nothingness along with a hint of motion.

Not the motion of a person or an animal. Rather, the motion of something falling down the fence.

For some reason, Sarah thought of an apple falling from a tree.

No tree stood there.

"Something's by the fence," whispered Sarah.

"Can you see it?"

"We have to get closer."

Now Sarah reached back and, with her free hand, caught the one Jill used to grip her. Hand in hand they edged forward not directly through the lawn but along the fence line. With their backs to this friendly obstacle, this simultaneous cause of privacy and isolation, the girls navigated around the perimeter of the dark yard and pressed against the edge of the shed.

"We should be ready to fight," Sarah whispered to Jill.

Her intense expression legible even in the almost total darkness beyond the flashlight's beam, Jill nodded once. She brandished the blade demonstratively.

"On three," whispered Jill. "One..."

Sarah, in time with her, chanted, "Two..."

"Three!"

Releasing one another's hands, Jill and Sarah leapt

around the corner of the shed.

They had been prepared for anything except the sight of Jack's dismembered corpse.

14.

WHILE JACK'S scream had been loud as it was long, the scream Jill and Sarah shared to discover the bisected boy was surely one that echoed through the neighborhood.

Jill bent to vomit her liquor into the grass. Sarah, in absolute shock, swept the flashlight beam over the terrible tableau.

The motion that had first caught her eye was, Sarah divined, some organ falling out of the body to join its fellows on the ground.

That was what it looked like amid the chaos of Jack's severed legs, at any rate. Hard to distinguish one part from another when everything was just a pile of meat.

Everything from the pelvis down had been seemingly torn away. Now, like a hideous anatomical model, the remaining internal organs of the body hung against the fence. Somehow the entire weight of Jack's upper half was supported by nothing more than a screwdriver.

Unable to stand the sight of the desecrated body and now too dissociated to realize what she was doing, Sarah stepped forward, gripped the handle of the screwdriver, and pulled it out with an audible *slorp.*

The noise produced another gag in Jill. Both girls screamed again, shorter cries, while the body dropped into the pile of its organs.

Somehow, the notion that Jack was dead didn't truly reach Sarah until that second. The same second that a twig snapped near the adjacent fence line.

The beam from the flashlight swept in the direction of the noise. It illuminated the figure so briefly that neither one of the girls even had time to make out its face before they booked it back to the house.

Jill screamed the whole way but Sarah didn't have the frame of mind to scream with her. Not until they reached the back door and the knob refused to give.

"It's *locked? It's locked?* Sarah! Sarah! What the fuck!"

"Fuck these stupid one-way locks! Billy! Billy! Billy! Let us in!"

Both girls screamed and pounded rapidly on the back door, fists banging in a fast timpani while the heavy footsteps of the figure closed in. While Jill continued pounding, Sarah whipped around with the screwdriver in one hand and the flashlight in the other.

She couldn't feel her face—couldn't feel anything but the white rush of terror as, inexorable and somehow alarmingly fast, the pursuing man emerged from the darkness and into the short beam of the flashlight.

Sarah screamed again, a sound so high and sharp that her throat strained beneath the urgency. That terrible clown mask from the crawlspace obscured his face, but Sarah knew who this this towering man with the rusted old kitchen knife had to be.

"Burr," cried Sarah, falling backward into the house as Billy at last responded to their screams and Jill rushed through the door.

Together the girls yanked the screen closed, then slammed shut the main door. They tested the lock and panted against the jamb for only a few seconds.

The boy, noticing neither the knife in Jill's hand nor the bloody screwdriver in Sarah's, asked, "Why'd you wake me up again? How come you turned the hall light off? It's so dark."

"Come on," whispered Sarah. She shifted both flashlight and screwdriver to one hand, then used the other to grab Billy's shoulder. "You need to hide, Billy. You need to hide right now."

Real alarm filled the boy's face in an instant. "Why?"

"Because we said so," hissed Jill, not quite so good with kids when under pressure.

In a moment of divine inspiration, Sarah told her

young charge, "Because—because the bogeyman is here."

The boy gasped in horror, his face transmuting into an expression of childish terror. The furrow of his brow was heartbreaking, but Sarah would rather he be afraid of the bogeyman than traumatized by the knowledge that a literal spree killer had come to re-live his peak crime. "Is he real?"

Sarah nodded rapidly. "He is. He's really, really real"—the girls exchanged an urgent glance as the screen door squeaked on the other side of the heavier, locked one—"and you have to hide, okay? You have to go hide until we come back and get you, and you can't make a sound."

"Okay," whispered Billy, looking more wide-eyed by the second.

Her hand tightening around his shoulder, Sarah dragged the boy down the dark hall. Jill was fast on their tail as Sarah guided him through the living room and to the stairs by the front of the house.

The small bookshelf—and the tiny crawlspace it had once concealed—was just in sight when the sound of shattering glass echoed from the kitchen.

"Hurry," whispered Sarah. She doubled her pace, ignoring the boy's cry as she practically pulled his arm from the socket. "Come on, Billy, hurry—get in there! Be careful—oh, be so careful, buddy—"

"Are the police coming?"

"Eventually," lied Sarah, throwing open the tiny

door and more or less stuffing the boy inside. "Get in the back. Get as far back there as you can possibly get. If somebody comes to find you and it's not one of us, you stay back. Don't let them come anywhere near you, not even if they say they're a cop."

"What if they can reach me?"

"Then you bite and kick and do whatever you can. Are you in there? Okay. Okay, buddy. Just wait—"

"It's so dark," complained the boy, his voice a pained whine.

Eyes squeezing briefly shut, Sarah said, "I know," before forcing herself to yield the flashlight. "Here, Billy, use this to keep it light in there. Just—just don't shine it on the door, okay? Keep the beam far away from the door all the time. As far away as you can. Do you know where your dad keeps his gun cabinet key?"

At a question like that the boy's brow furrowed with far greater intensity. He shook his head at first. Sarah began to close the door until he said, "Wait—"

She cracked it an inch and peered in at him. "Before he goes shooting, Daddy goes into the basement. He goes there when he comes back from shooting, too."

With a sharp breath of gratitude, Sarah nodded and said, "Okay, okay, that's perfect, Billy, thank you! Oh—you're such a smart kid, thank you—"

Then, in the darkness, Sarah stood upright and slammed the crawlspace shut. Breath held, she tugged the squat bookshelf back into place and was grateful for Jill's help.

They'd gotten it set before the door for all of one full second before the thunder of footsteps through the living room sent Jill fleeing up the stairs, tripping over one and cursing her friend by the next.

"Why did you have to give him the fucking flash-light," whispered Jill as Sarah scrambled behind her in the dark.

"I don't know, dude. I don't know—I had to! He's just a kid. I can't let him be scared in there."

"He's going to be scared no matter what, doofus! What the fuck are we going to do now?"

"We have to find a way to get into that gun cabinet. You heard what Billy said."

"Then we're going the wrong way." Despondent, Jill looked over her shoulder and back toward the stairs. "We're about to be trapped up here."

Maybe—or maybe not. In the darkness it was diffi-cult for Sarah to make out the details of anything, but certain shapes were still evident. Paintings hanging on the walls lost their meaning, but their silhouettes stood out.

The same was true of the second-floor laundry chute.

Without hesitation, Sarah dropped to her knees and used the bloody screwdriver still gripped in her hand to hastily work out the screws of the chute. "You can't be serious," whispered Jill. "He's coming—dude, what are you doing?"

"We can get to the basement through here! We'll have to squeeze—"

"There's no *way I* can fit down there! You tiny bitch." Jill's eyes widened at the slamming shut of a coat closet door. He was looking for them. "Oh, shit! Give me that—"

Snatching the screwdriver from Sarah's clumsier hand, Jill whizzed through the other two screws at a speed almost inhuman.

The drawer of the laundry chute fell open like a shocked mouth. Together, they yanked it clear of the wall.

A black hole stared them down.

Sarah bent her head to peer inside.

"No," said Jill, her face feral with terror as Sarah looked back up. "No way. I'm not even going to try."

"I have to," insisted Sarah, leaning her head in. With some wiggling and twisting of the sort that had permitted her to lean into the crawlspace, her shoulders managed to fit inside, too.

Downstairs, the first stair creaked beneath the weight of its old and most despised owner.

Jill's gasp sounded like it wanted to be a scream, or maybe a sob. "Oh my God! He's coming—Sarah, you have to hurry! Can you fit?"

"This is such a long drop—" Anxiety filled her. Sarah lifted her head out to turn herself around and try to slide down feet-first.

Her expression tight, Sarah braced herself against

the narrow chute so as not to freefall down. At the same time, she extended her hand and gripped Jill's.

"I'll be right back," she swore to her friend.

Something in this sentence changed Jill's face. As if she realized something terrible.

Jill squeezed Sarah, then released her to shove her down into the chute with an unceremonious hand on the top of her skull.

"Just get that key, dude. Get that key, get that gun, get the fuck out of here."

The last thing Sarah saw before falling down the chute was the awful grimace of the clown mask behind Jill's head.

15.

PETITE THOUGH she was, Sarah found the laundry chute to be a terror in her own right. It was a tight fit, and as she wiggled down she wondered if the already narrow chamber would remain its current width or if it would narrow even more at the base.

Well...at least, if that were the case, Burr was going to have a hell of a time getting to her before she died of asphyxiation.

What was he doing here? All the people he'd killed—had that all been in the name of getting to his old house? Why?

Sarah couldn't fathom it, but she tried to. It was something to focus on other than the claustrophobic chute she'd entered without a guaranteed means of exit.

Thankfully, fate was on her side in at least one way.

Much as dishes stacked up in the Johnsons' sink, laundry piled at the bottom of the chute. As Sarah pushed one foot through the opening, she contacted a pile of clothes.

Yes! Yes, she was almost out.

A bit more maneuvering was required, but soon she carefully lowered herself down into the absolute darkness of the Johnsons' basement. For a few seconds of shocked relief, she burst into tears.

What was even going on?

This was supposed to be a normal night. A night like any other. She was supposed to put the kid to bed, get paid, go home. Instead—instead, she had endangered the lives of two people by roping them into her gig.

Actually, scratch that. She caused the death of the boy she liked. All because she gave into Jill's peer pressure and ended up stupidly inviting him over.

Was it really Jill's fault, though?

Sarah ran her fingertips over her shut eyelids and forced herself to stop her crying.

Forget that self-blame shit! Sarah didn't cause anybody's death. Millions of babysitters all over the world called their boyfriends over the very second their clients were out of the house. Those babysitters didn't have to deal with the ramifications of homicide.

It wasn't Sarah's fault that this was happening. It was Burr's. It was Monroe State Hospital. It was anybody's. Anybody's but hers.

But that didn't mean Sarah had to be a helpless victim. She was going to do her job, damn it. She was hired to be a babysitter. That meant it was her job to look after Billy like he was her own.

And she'd do it. No way in hell was she going to let Neoklaus Burr or anybody else harm a hair on that kid's head.

And no way was she going to die that night, either.

Having resolved that she would survive this no matter the cost, Sarah extended her hands and moved into the darkness of the Johnsons' basement.

Her palms navigated the unfamiliar territory for her as best they could.

It was like being blind! Yes. Just like that. She tried to reassure herself. If blind people could move through a world they'd never seen and live as functional adults, Sarah could move through the darkness without fear—without knocking something over and attracting the killer.

Though she did come dangerously close, once or twice, to doing just that.

Her finger, for instance, brushed a paint can perched precariously upon a stack of cardboard boxes. It shifted toward the limit of its security like a human contemplating suicide on a bridge. Sarah held her breath, felt down around the cardboard box, and gently eased the can back into place before moving on.

The uncanny cellar of the house seemed to be arranged in several rooms, though it was hard to tell because it was so dark. However, as she navigated through the obscurity, her hand grazed a wooden beam. A doorway?

Peering up through the almost impenetrable blackness, Sarah confirmed that she stood under the threshold between two rooms. Then, while marveling that her eyes had adjusted so quickly to such thick darkness, she noticed the barest hint of blue light.

Moonlight.

Yes! Yes! There was a window here somewhere.

In fact, that might have been the best way out. Ah...if she could just use the same small size that had permitted her to squeeze down that laundry chute, then she would be in the clear. She could wiggle out through the window and escape! Get help!

And leave Jill and Billy behind.

Miserable, Sarah emerged in the only subterranean room bathed in the moon's blue light. She crossed her arms against the creepy feeling of the basement, amazed she could still feel spooked by inanimate darkness when a killer lurked around the house.

A killer lurked around the house. She reminded herself of that and hurried into the room.

First, Sarah nudged a few mildewed boxes of old sports supplies against the wall. She used these to boost herself up and check the window out, grimacing—and not just at the instability of the cardboard beneath her feet.

This window was pretty small, even for her. Its well was concrete, meaning that forcing herself through and somehow digging her way out of the edge of the Johnson's lawn wasn't really an option. The only way back up was going to be by the stairs, and that implied a whole host of other problems she was too afraid to consider.

She had to focus on what she could control.

She had come down here not to escape but for something else. Just to get the key.

Yes, right.

Just look for a tiny gun cabinet key in a dark basement, Sarah.

No big deal.

Sarah squeezed her eyes shut, one hand on her forehead and her lips pursed tight. Okay. Okay. The liquor cabinet key had been stuffed into a record sleeve. Maybe the gun cabinet key was hidden similarly?

In the pale light of the window, Sarah struggled to parse the individual objects making up the sea of clutter.

The workbench against the wall was arrayed with items relating to Mrs. Johnson's craft hobbies: the origin of the overflowing materials stuffed in an empty drawer of Mr. Johnson's far more organized office.

Shuffling through this desk's contents yielded nothing. In fact, the sewing machine was so covered in dust that Sarah wondered if Mrs. Johnson had sewn anything in years.

However...this fruitless search was not without its merits. With the help of the moonlight and a few seemingly wasted minutes of precious time, Sarah's eyes had adjusted further.

First she noticed a sharp-looking pair of bolt cutters. Gleaming, seldom-used, neat in comparison to other messy gardening supplies piled on the same wooden shelf.

Then, as though the bolt cutters were a helpful arrow arranged by the beneficent house itself, Sarah followed the point of blades that seemed to indicate a pile of neglected VHS tapes.

Sarah's hope was born again as she hurried over. The liquor cabinet key in its record sleeve—oh, this had to be it.

Mr. Johnson was exactly the sort of person who thought he was being clever by developing some sort of theme for where he hid his keys. He was a wise guy who routinely started projects like the refurbished car before leaving them to languish: the sort of too-clever dad who would make his safe combination Billy's birthday and be shocked when a burglar robbed him blind.

But just then, sorting through the VHS tapes, Sarah was grateful—immensely grateful—for that smug quality of Mr. Johnson's.

These were apparently the movies the Johnsons deemed too scary to keep upstairs in the office where

Billy could readily access them. Squinting to read their labels, Sarah made out titles like *Alien, Jaws* and *The Shining.* As one may have gathered from the horror movie posters in his office, Mr. Johnson was a dedicated film buff who had wasted no time collecting his horror favorites as soon as home video became an option.

That was why, amid this sequestered collection, *Mary Poppins* caught Sarah's eye.

The Disney movie had nothing to do with horror, was totally Billy-appropriate, and therefore would have bored the morbid Johnson boy to tears. It was natural that an unwatched movie would be moved downstairs, but this one in particular was so ill-suited to its surroundings—and, somehow, so thematically appropriate—that Sarah lunged for it as soon as she noticed it.

Unlike its fellows, it was not dust-covered. That was perhaps the real detail that earned her notice, albeit subconsciously. Whatever the reason, as soon as Sarah picked it up she felt the same tiny deformation of cardboard that had called Jill's attention to the Coleman vinyl.

Breath held, Sarah turned the sleeve over. She shook the tape into her hand and gasped with ecstasy as a tiny key fell out along with it.

Okay.

Okay.

Step one.

Now...step two?
The basement door opened.
Sarah had no more time to think.

16.

THE HUMAN heart can sound almost impossibly loud to its owner in a time of duress. This fact was a cruel irony. Oh, the very breath required to live had surely doomed more than one person in a situation similar to Sarah's.

Then again, how many people found themselves in a situation like this? Trapped in the basement of an employer's house while a killer lumbered steadily down the stairs?

Silently as she'd ever moved in her life, Sarah pocketed the key. She moved slowly as she lifted the bolt cutters from the nearby shelf. After sweeping her eyes along the room and seeing the appearance of a foot upon the distant stair, Sarah covered the shining blades with her hand.

Holding the bolt cutters to her breast as though

they were a child to protect, Sarah ducked between a wall and the box of VHS tapes. There, she willed her breath to remain silent and steady.

Had Burr heard her move? At the bottom of the stairs those heavy footfalls seemed to pause.

Sarah's eyes shut briefly, but fear and readiness forced them open again. While adrenaline hammered at high speed through her every vein, she braced herself where she knelt. She focused.

The footsteps started again.

Her stomach twisted in absolute terror. This was bad. Oh, this was so bad. If he saw her, it was all over. She'd die alone in the Johnsons' basement.

And what would happen to Billy? Would anybody find him? When the cops came to finally take a look at the crime scene, would they hear his screams from the same crawlspace the cops in 1960 had neglected to thoroughly check?

No. Sarah couldn't rely on cops. She couldn't rely on anybody but herself and the bolt cutters clasped in her hand, hidden away to keep them from reflecting even the faintest beam of moonlight.

The same can of paint that Sarah had pushed back into place fell from its station on Burr's passage. The killer stopped in place while the can rolled across the floor, oozing white primer and producing a surface that was marginally more reflective than the unfinished floor of gray concrete.

God! Don't let him see her. Don't let him look right.

Let him stay focused on someplace, anyplace else.

Burr's steady footsteps resumed around the puddle of white paint.

It took Sarah every ounce of self-control to avoid gasping at his appearance. The red boiler suit he wore, faded though it was, somehow made him seem the very devil—though, that effect could have just as easily been evoked by the knife he clutched in his hand.

The knife that, Sarah noticed, was reddened. Shining. Not with rust or an old, dried stain but a very fresh, very real coating of red blood.

Jill.

Sarah squeezed her eyes shut and cursed herself for abandoning her friend. If only she'd stayed behind with Jill! Then—

Then they would have died together.

Was that really so much better than Sarah taking a chance to survive?

And, anyway, there was no telling whose blood that was. For all Sarah knew, it was Jack's. Jill could have been perfectly fine—or, if not fine, perhaps she had at least survived the stabbing. Sarah had to find her and see.

But first, she had to get out of the basement and away from this towering killer in a clown mask.

There was only one chance that she could see. She wasn't going to be able to sneak past him, but she couldn't just wait around, either. The longer Burr lingered in the basement, the more his eyes would adjust just like hers had. His seeing her crouched there between the box and the wall was a matter of time.

She was going to have to run.

The notion occurred to her with a kind of animal specificity. A voice screaming in her mind. It bloomed in her as Burr emerged in the cellar's final room, and it had risen to the level of an emergency siren by the time he stopped before the wall to study the same window Sarah had.

He stood there in silence, perhaps deciding whether or not his prey had managed to squeeze through. His back was to her.

RUN.

At once it was the only word in Sarah's head. As she leapt up, her foot nudged the box. There was no time to cringe. Burr turned in her periphery while, without sparing him a glance, Sarah let her arms fall to her sides and pumped them amid her sprint.

Had there been time, she might have applauded her own sudden Olympic potential. That was quite a leap she made over the white puddle of primer—and it was safe to say that, if she had managed to reach speeds like this during gym class, Sarah might have enjoyed physical education a little more.

Burr was pretty fast, himself. His long legs permitted him to catch up with his quarry at an alarming pace: Sarah quite literally cried out to realize how soon he gained ground.

By the time she mounted the stairs, he was no more than a foot behind her. She sobbed while his knife slashed dangerously near her Achilles tendon.

Keep going! Just keep going. Her arms outstretched, Sarah burst through the basement door and careened into the main floor of the house. So disoriented that she wasn't even sure where she'd emerged, she just threw the door shut behind her and bolted off through the twists of the dark Johnson house.

She took every corner, jetted down every hall, often selected the only options available to her—and somehow, amid this panic, she found herself back upstairs.

There was no time to think. Burr's pursuit was truly unending and she heard him on the stairs already. Unable to reach the master bedroom without trapping herself, Sarah ducked into Billy's open bedroom, hurried into his closet, and concealed herself among his clothes.

Those footsteps again. Sarah urged her breathing to soften as Burr paused in the upstairs hall. It was as though she could hear him thinking—as though the house's atmosphere took on a darker, deeper vibration when his brain worked on problems not related to the immediate butchery of a human being.

Issues like hunting and cornering said human being, required some nuance, after all. Something more than the base animal-consciousness with which the sharklike killer was imbued. When it came to such matters, Sarah wasn't sure that he was exceptionally bright. Could a being who existed only for murder really be expected to problem-solve?

Fear surged in her again as his footsteps penetrated Billy's room. Again, they stopped. She could feel him looking—wondering. It occurred to Sarah that he may not even have realized a child lived in the house until that very moment. Had she been where she couldn't be heard, she would have cursed.

Great.

Now he knew Billy existed. Now he knew he had to really *look f*or someone beyond the teenager he violently dogged.

Those footsteps trailed toward the bed, whose metal frame and hand-me-down twin mattress groaned beneath the easy lifting of his hand.

Finding nothing beneath, Burr let the bed drop again.

Sarah leaned her head back against the wall. Thank God they'd hidden Billy where they had! If they'd sent him off to hide on his own, who knew what might have happened. Secure that the boy was not likely to be found in his current location, Sarah could, if nothing else, focus on her own survival...and on getting back with Jill.

She was getting ahead of herself, though. Before anything else, she had to get out of that closet. She had to be ready to fight at a second's notice. No longer needing to protect the reflective blades from moonlight, Sarah uncovered the bolt cutters readied herself to use the unwieldy gardening tool as a makeshift means to stab her pursuer.

It looked like she might have to. His steps echoed across the room, louder each foot he drew nearer to the closet. The door groaned in misery as it cracked open and Sarah, breath held, became still as a statue.

Burr stepped into the closet.

A few of Billy's shirts shifted as the broad man brushed past them. He and Sarah were inches apart, though it seemed Burr didn't realize it. Yes: Sarah could have reached out and touched the killer's leg. Could have taken him by surprise and stabbed him right then, for whatever good it would do.

But just as the urge to run had been so clear in her head, the pressure to stay perfectly still was all she felt now.

It wasn't worth taking a risk here. He quite literally had the high ground. Crouched as she was amid the clothes, she could have nicked him in the leg, sure—but just imagine the leverage he'd have when he bent down and started stabbing her. Her mind filled up with terrible intrusive images, simulations of her own possible deaths if she made so much as one wrong move.

'Possible' deaths, though. Only possible. Not guaranteed.

Nothing was guaranteed. Even though Burr stood so close to her in the dark closet, his seeing her was far from a guarantee.

And he didn't.

Somehow, he didn't.

He walked to the end of the closet. Burr opened the door to the adjoining bedroom, intended to be a sibling's quarters but, in the Johnsons' only-child home, relegated to a guest room. Burr's footfall thumped through this second bedroom, then paused again.

Again, the sound of a bed being lifted. Again, the sound of a bed being dropped.

At last he walked away, opened the door, and left the room to try elsewhere in the upstairs hall.

Sarah released her held breath and stared up at the ceiling in unspeakable gratitude.

Having maintained an almost incomprehensible degree of stillness against the onslaught of so much adrenaline, her body burst into a fit of tremors. The shaking was violent enough to chatter her teeth. She took an extra second to try to get it to stop.

Sarah couldn't relax yet, though. Couldn't celebrate; couldn't let herself feel fear.

She had to pay attention. Sarah leaned forward, ears primed to catch every slightest sound that reverberated through the upstairs floor.

That was how she heard Burr's steps lead around the hallway. Then, at a slower pace, down the staircase of the house.

That was how she heard the stairs squeak, as if in protest of Burr's vile intentions.

That was how, even several rooms away, Sarah detected a low, almost inhuman moan that sounded just a little like Jill.

17.

STILL ALIVE?

Jill was still alive?

Perhaps it was incredible to think that Jill had been trapped on the same floor as Neoklaus Burr and not been met with instant death, but that was what Sarah discovered.

Once she heard the distinctive cry of the bottom stair and its attached landing, Sarah rose from her hiding place and slipped out into Billy's room.

The bed now sat crookedly away from the wall, its mattress having bounced askew upon its box spring once Burr dropped it. Shuddering at the ease with which the man had lifted the bed frame—he hadn't so much as grunted with the exertion, if it could have been called 'exertion' at all—Sarah crept into the hall and listened again.

This time she listened not for Burr's steps, but for Jill's voice.

Soon, she was rewarded. Another moan drifted pitifully up through the second floor of the Johnsons' despoiled home. Sarah pursued it in silence and discovered the master bedroom door cracked open.

Braced for the worst, Sarah pushed open the door and winced at the beginnings of a squeak she aborted by stopping the motion mid-swing. Instead of opening the door any further, she exhaled and squeezed through the gap.

That exhalation transformed into an immediate gasp on seeing her friend arranged in a bloody heap upon the Johnson's master bed.

The sight was so horrible that, if it hadn't been Jill, Sarah wouldn't have looked at all. But she had to look. She had to see the friend she'd brought here.

The friend who, Sarah now confirmed, was doomed to die. All because she had come to soothe Sarah's fears.

It felt like a human sacrifice.

"Sarah?" Jill's voice was a wet rasp: one accented by a terrible gurgle that was more harrowing than even her moans through the hall. "Oh, Sarah...you've got to get out of here."

"I can't just leave *Billy* here—I can't leave you here, either. Hold on, let me see."

Somewhere, amid the layers of blood still flowing from Jill's gut, Sarah made out the star shape of a reddened hand. Gingerly as she could, Sarah lifted that limp hand and tried not to gasp out loud at the overflowing stab wounds that peppered her friend's abdomen.

While it was hard to tell how many there were, especially through the fabric of Jill's stained shirt, Sarah couldn't help but guess that there had to be more than—what, ten, twenty?

Sarah had no experience with things like this, but it didn't take an expert in modern forensics to tell the unlucky teenager from 1982 that Burr was a sick son of a bitch. He had absolutely mutilated Jill's body with the rusty knife he'd taken out of the garbage.

Sarah's hand tightened around her friend's to see what had been done to her.

"It's pretty fucking gnarly, huh, dude?" Jill tried to laugh, but moaned in agony as her stomach warped with the sound. "Oh! Fuck, ugh, I feel like my organs are on fire! Can you see them? Can you see my organs?"

Only distantly aware by this point of how awful it was to have to say such a thing, Sarah shook her head. "No, I can't—I can't see them. Maybe if we can get you to a hospital—"

"You dumb bitch, no way! Don't fucking worry about me. Worry about yourself." Suddenly hopeful, her remaining ounces of strength permitting her hand to clench like a vise around Sarah's, Jill whispered, "Did you get the key to the gun cabinet?"

Amid Burr's pursuit and now this terrible discovery, Sarah had practically forgotten. Setting down the bolt cutters still gripped in her free hand, she removed the tiny key from her pocket and held it before Jill's struggling eyes. Those foggy orbs lit up a little, a faint smile twitching across her lips.

"You're a fucking champ, Sarah. Fuck! You're such a badass. Kill that son of a bitch for me—don't ever let him do something like this to anybody else. Don't let him touch you."

"I won't. I promise, I wont."

"That's good. If you let that psycho hurt a hair on your head, I'll come back as a ghost to haunt your ass."

Laughing weakly, Sarah released her friend's hand and turned away to get the cabinet opened. "You can't haunt me if you're not dead, so just don't die...maybe if I can get Billy and we can get out of here, we can get you help in time."

"Maybe this fucker will be the next Pope," whispered Jill.

Sarah yanked open the cabinet door.

With an appreciative throb of love for America and its sacred second amendment, Sarah beheld the array of pistols, rifles, and other weapons within. While she snatched out the only weapon she had a hope of using without losing—namely, a reasonably sized pistol— her friend went on to ask, "Is it loaded?"

"I don't know. How do I check?"

"Oh my God, are you kidding? You're so fucked."

While a chill swept through Sarah at her friend's cruel teasing, Jill extended her hand and weakly said, "Here, give it here."

Though she set the gun in Jill's hand, it began to slip from her loose grip. Sarah found she had to quite literally close her friend's fist around the handle to secure the transfer.

With its grip fit to her bloody palm, Jill hefted the gun toward her face, barrel pointed away. She used her slightly more functioning hand to examine the muzzle, then check the chamber.

"No. Not a round. Fuck responsible gun ownership, man..." Passing the weapon back to Sarah, Jill lamented, "You'll have to find ammo. Can you figure out how to load it? You have to do what I just did, kind of... Christ! I'm so fucked up, I can't even explain."

"Don't worry. I'll figure it out. I have to figure out where the ammo is, after all...I have to figure out a lot."

While the girls shared a humorless laugh, Jill suddenly produced an agonized sound of revelation. "Oh—my car...take my car, Sarah."

Hope flooded the babysitter to hear this suggestion. Of course! Jill's car. "Where are your keys?"

"In my purse downstairs on the—on the end table, oh—"

Jill's facade collapsed beneath the pressure of her pain. She rolled upon her side, groaning and twisting to fend off the agony. "Fuck, ah, Sarah! Sarah, I'm scared."

"I know, Jill. Oh, man, dude, I know. But it'll be okay. Okay? We'll get you out. You just have to hang in there for me."

"Okay," whispered Jill, staring muggily into her friend's face. "But if I don't...just make sure this fucker dies."

She'd do her best.

"Keep these bolt cutters for now," Sarah said to her friend. "If he comes back, you can take him by surprise."

"Oh yeah," said Jill, sarcastic to the end. "Totally. I'm in great condition to do that. I'll just hop up with these stupid bolt cutters and stick 'em right in his thick skull...yeah, I'll be an action movie hero. They'll make documentaries about me. Fuck you, Sarah."

"Kiss my ass, Jill."

"You've always been a—a total bitch."

"Takes one to know one."

Sarah looked over her shoulder seconds before leaving the room.

She exchanged a smile with her already grinning friend, then squeezed through the gap of the door.

With the empty pistol stuffed into the waistband of her pants, Sarah left her friend behind in the Johnson's master bedroom. Planting each step with steady deliberation, she secreted herself in the nearby bathroom.

A second flashlight, one that was stronger but far

more unwieldy, sat on the edge of the in-renovation sink. Sarah had just picked it up and turned it on when the familiar sound of Burr's foot upon the stairs triggered a new spell of panic.

There was no time to squeeze down into the laundry chute. Frankly, she'd only had time for that in the first place because Jill had been there to play backup.

Left to fend for herself against this home invader, Sarah stepped into the hall and analyzed her options.

She found them sorely lacking. Windows seemed to be the only way out in a pinch. Sarah had to be willing to jump and tried quickly to picture the house from the outside.

The upstairs den overlooked the street. Maybe she could hop down from the porch roof and minimize the risk of injury.

But what if the doors locked her out again? Then it would be Billy alone. In the crawlspace, maybe, but still trapped in the house with that monster.

The vacant eyes of the clown mask appeared, heralding the rest of Burr's massive red frame.

She'd pondered too long.

Sarah's heart felt encased in a block of ice. Dizzy with terror, she decided to try the den anyway.

The babysitter wasted no time. She dashed into the room that, in so many ways, had already significantly extended her life due to its turntable and liquor cabinet.

Yes! If not for the liquor cabinet, Jack never would

have showed up. It was horrible that he died, but his death had alerted Sarah and Jill to the presence of the killer. The friendly liquor cabinet had been what really lured the boy over.

And, seeing as the heights from the window were far more expansive than she'd hoped, Sarah thought that the cabinet might just have one more way to save her.

While Burr's steps quaked the house along his path to the den, Sarah pushed the heavy cabinet away from the wall a few inches. With this space available, she squeezed behind to push it out a little more. The glass-fronted antique groaned dangerously.

Sarah clutched the wooden backing to keep it upright as long as possible. Just until—

Burr stepped into the room.

As soon as the killer was in that cramped den with Sarah, her true sense of urgency set in. The atoms of her brain screamed with panic while she applied every ounce of strength in all four of her limbs.

Sarah rammed the cabinet forward.

The unwieldy display piece was not made for such stress. The foremost pair of hand-carved legs snapped under the pressure.

Burr's head whipped around.

Too late, fucker.

Sarah guessed that mask interfered with his peripheral vision. Burr was crushed beneath a rain of shattering glass even before the hefty oak backing of the cabinet, a single solid piece that did the brunt of the damage, landed flat upon him with a painful *thud.*

Once it settled, both killer and cabinet were still.

A normal person would have cried out when crushed like that. Sarah would only later realize that Burr never made a sound. At the time, she was in such an urgent state of automated fight-or-flight response that she didn't notice.

Sarah's one and only thought was of escape.

She didn't stop to gloat or to investigate if he was dead. Sarah simply mounted the wooden back of the cabinet.

In its collapse it had come to take up most of the room. The door to the den opened inward: Sarah grimaced to realize it was blocked by the wreckage.

Leaping nimbly from the cabinet to land in the small space of floor still available beside the door, Sarah yanked it open with all her might. The doorknob jamming into her ribs, she began contort her body through.

Burr's massive hand shot from beneath the cabinet and grabbed her right ankle.

18.

SARAH'S HIGH scream was instant and but one of several noises that immediately rang through the room. The tinkling of glass and the groan of the cabinet amid Burr's movement was another.

The sound of her foot, kicking that hand as hard as it could against the edge of the rattling cabinet, was the backbeat to it all. A flat, hard, thumping rhythm, sometimes punctuated by a crunch.

When the hand still failed to release her, she drew the pistol from the back of her pants. Sarah whipped its handle hard across Burr's knuckles. Once, twice— three times, until the instant bruising beneath the metallic onslaught had begun to purple his swelling fingers.

Only when his body's nerves forced him to release his grip did he at last submit.

The haunting image of his hand slowly sliding back under the upended liquor cabinet was the last thing Sarah saw in the den. She withdrew her foot, shut the door, and sprinted down the stairs as fast as she could.

The adrenaline pounding through her—and the exertion required for a small girl to push over such a heavy liquor cabinet—left all her limbs trembling with unspent energy. The child's bookshelf before the crawlspace door was easier to shove aside than ever.

While she yanked open the door with one hand, Sarah re-holstered the gun down the back of her jeans. Urgently, she whisper-cried, "Billy, it's me, hurry, come out—come out right now—"

Thankfully the boy was equally primed with adrenaline.

Billy sprang out of the crawlspace, the flashlight still in his hand. "Did you kill the bogeyman?"

"Not yet. We still have to be super careful. I need you to listen to everything I tell you. Come on, follow me. Come on, Billy—"

Snatching the kid in her arms weighed her down considerably, no matter how light he was: but carrying him was still faster than tugging him along. With Billy on her hip, Sarah rushed into the living room, immediately set eyes on her friend's open purse, and reached a hand inside. The keys were the first thing she brushed and she kissed them when she picked them up.

"Okay," said Sarah, "okay, okay—"

"Where's Jill? Where's Jack?"

"Oh, honey—let's go, okay? Let's go, and we'll talk later—"

Completely out of breath, arms weak, Sarah nonetheless pushed onward. The boy, seeming to sense her weakness, shifted his grip on her. He now clamped his arms around her neck, an action that helped her considerably. As Sarah rushed back to the hall and shoved open the front door, Billy glanced down.

"Is that your blood? Are you bleeding?"

"Don't worry, okay? Don't worry. I'm fine. We're both going to be fine." Sarah's lungs turned inside-out as, upstairs, there echoed a heavy rattle that was punctuated by a thump.

With a roll of eyes that instantly glazed in angry tears, Sarah shoved open the front door.

Without bothering to close it behind her, she ran down the lawn. Jill's car sat parked along the side of the road.

"Okay—okay. Okay, Billy, let's get you settled in, come on—"

After unlocking the passenger door, Sarah extricated herself from the kid's steel grip and shoved him inside.

She shut the door after him, darted around to the driver's side, and scrambled in behind the wheel.

Sarah crammed the key into the ignition.

Jill's car didn't start.

"What the fuck," whispered Sarah, slamming down the brake while twisting the key. "What the fuck, what the fuck—"

"That's a bad word—"

Sarah slammed her hands on the steering wheel, her eyes blind with the burning of her tears. "Please shut up, Billy! Please! Shut up and let me think!"

To her later shame, she had screamed at the kid. It was understandable given the circumstances. At that point in time, however, she felt not an iota of guilt. Her high pitch only made her wonder why no one had come to help her.

Of course, when her frustrated mind posited the question, she provided her own answer in a second.

Cops were out everywhere looking for Burr, dealing with his other murders, trying to prevent more. Meanwhile, civilians were being urged to stay inside. They were being told not to answer their doors for strangers.

They were being told not to get involved.

If Sarah ran away screaming and pounded on every shut door in the neighborhood, no one—not a soul—would have emerged to help her.

Sarah couldn't expect anybody to get her—them—through this. Nobody would help her. She had to help herself.

Body numb by now with all the stress hormones flooding its fibers, Sarah leapt from the car and rushed to the hood.

She didn't have to pop it to know they'd been sabotaged: the flashlight highlighted red bloodstains. Thick fingerprints imprinted upon the hood of Jill's white car.

Motion flickered near the façade of the house. Nauseous, Sarah looked up.

Burr had filled the open door frame.

"Fuck! Oh, fuck. Oh, God—Billy—come here—"

Jerking open the driver's side door, Sarah urged the boy to crawl across the center console. When he had, she asked him, "How fast can you run?"

"Fast," insisted Billy, nodding. "Really fast."

"Okay. Okay. What I want you to do is, when I say 'go,' I want you to run around the back of the car"— her eyes flickered up as Burr began to move toward them and she grabbed Billy's shoulders to keep him from following her gaze back to the killer—"up the lawn, and right into the house. Don't stop until you get in the garage. Is the car in there locked?"

The boy shook his head and she said, "Okay—okay meet me in there—stop!"

Sarah whipped the empty gun out of her waistband and pointed it at the killer who by then was a few feet from the inoperable vehicle.

For just a second—almost literally a second, maybe two—he did pause.

Sarah stepped out around the left side of the car and gestured with the gun as though ready to shoot. She even remembered to pull the hammer back.

Burr resumed his steady pace.

Her stomach lurched as the distance between them closed. Sarah's eyes locked not on the hideous clown face but the reddened knife in his huge hand.

"Go," screamed Sarah, leaping back a few feet in preparation for her own sprint around the perimeter of the car.

It was so gratifying to watch Billy bolt into the house! Like a little blue comet—go, Billy, go!

She wanted to cheer but had no time.

Alerted by the noise of Billy's fast steps, the killer wheeled around. Watching Burr track the boy's path was like seeing a lion's attention link to the movement of a gazelle.

Somehow, this had the effect of enraging Sarah.

While the lumbering murderer turned toward the fleeing child—proving, as he did, as ill-suited to move about as the liquor cabinet had been—Sarah hurled Jill's useless keys at the back of his head. She feinted right, then dashed left.

The blade whizzed past the small of her back.

Sarah cried out, urging her muscles into the peak of action, begging her burning limbs to cooperate. She remembered her own advice to Billy: run and run and don't stop until you're in the garage. As she surged forward she told herself that same vital gem, but did delay just a moment. Just to slam the front door and hit the bolt.

"Find another way back in, asshole," she screamed

while dashing to the garage.

There it was: Mr. Johnson's dusty old car. Oh, she had never been so happy to see it. Shutting the garage door behind her, Sarah tried the driver's side. Her stomach sank.

Locked? Empty? Where was Billy?

Just as panic began to renew, the rear driver's side door flew open.

Billy leapt from under an old tarp he'd been smart enough to drag into the back of the car. "Sarah!"

"Oh dude! Little dude!" Sarah hugged him tight enough to crush him, saying, "I'm so glad to see you! Is the car still out of gas?"

The boy nodded rapidly. "But Dad keeps a big red can in the shed. That might have gas in it!"

"Okay. Okay. Any chance you know where he keeps the bullets for his guns?"

At that, Billy frowned. He shook his head.

This poor kid—his pupils were traumatized pinpoints and his eyes had circles from the simple exhaustion of spending such an extended period of time mortally afraid. She could relate.

Sarah patted him. "That's okay! You're the greatest, Billy. Such a smart kid—I'll be at your college graduation, just wait. Yeah, oh—you'll be, like, a doctor someday, wait and see! Now get in there, get back in there—"

The boy climbed into the car. At the last second, while tucking the tarp over him, Sarah asked, "I don't suppose your dad lets you know where he keeps his shed key, does he?"

Of course not. While the kid shook his head, Sarah sighed.

Looked like she was going to have to go back upstairs and get those bolt-cutters. Well...if nothing else, it was a good opportunity to grab Jill.

Assuming there was time, of course.

Sarah stepped out of the garage, her flashlight's beam no longer trembling but steady with the sheer intensity of her will to survive. The light flooded the hall.

As it did, the tinkle of glass rang out from the previously broken kitchen window.

Trying not to succumb to another fit of tearful frustration, Sarah switched off her flashlight and ran through the dark. Being acquainted with it as she was by now, she skipped that loud bottom stair and vaulted a few more before padding softly up the rest.

While, downstairs, Burr's steps retraced through the living room, Sarah crept to the master bedroom. She slipped again through the crack of the squeaking door.

Her eyes squeezed shut at the sight of Jill's body, the bolt cutters clutched limply in its hand.

"Jill," whispered Sarah, now unable to help a few searing tears. She stroked her friend's stiffly sprayed, blood-matted hair. "Oh, Jill! I'm so sorry."

"You fucking...should be...bitch..."

"Jill!" How quickly sorrow turned to hope! Restraining herself from gripping her wounded friend's shoulders, Sarah gasped to look into her friend's barely opened eyes. "Oh, Jill—you're alive—"

"And so tired...hurts so bad...fucking wish I were dead..."

"Don't say that! Please, don't say that. Come on, come with me. We're going to get the Johnsons' car gassed up and get out of here."

"What about *my car?*"

"I don't know. Burr sabotaged it somehow—"

"That fucker! Not enough to kill me...have to kill my car, too...what a son of a bitch..."

Groaning to be hauled upright in Sarah's trembling arms, Jill begged, "No, Sarah! Leave me here..."

"I can't let you just *die. It'll take five minutes to get the gas. Not even that. We'll be out of here in no time."*

"Yeah, right!"

"We will! I promise! I need you to just believe in me, okay?"

"Okay, Sarah...okay. Just don't—ugh, don't grab me there, ow—! Oh, ow..."

"Sorry, hold on—"

While adjusting her grip on Jill and clenching the blood-soaked bolt cutters with one hand, Sarah realized they couldn't fit through the squeaky bedroom door without pushing it open wider. Quiet as she may have been on her way upstairs, Burr was for sure going to hear that.

169

"We're going to have to move fast, okay? So just—just do your best, and remember, I've got you."

Before Sarah could shove wide the door with her foot, Burr opened it for her.

19.

WHAT HAPPENED next happened so fast, and was so much a series of physiological, instinctive responses to stimuli, that Sarah couldn't keep track of everything.

It somehow amazed her that she could feel with such vivid detail the bite of Burr's rusted knife as it slashed across her arm; amazed, too, that she managed to discern the tone of Jill's scream from her own.

What shocked Sarah most of all, though, was her ability to barrel past him, Jill in her arms.

Somehow, she forced herself to squeeze past the killer. Just as she had been wiggling in and out of the cracked door all this time.

Why was that so incredible to her? Only because it seemed as though mere contact with Burr should have somehow been the cause of some grave injury.

Yes, as if simply brushing shoulders with him should have ended her very life.

But Burr was not some supernatural creature. Not that Sarah could tell, anyway.

Just a man. A huge man.

Practically a demon, yes.

But only practically.

In reality, he was made of flesh and bone. Not fire and brimstone. And he could slash her, even stab her with that knife of his, but it didn't matter.

As long as she kept moving, Burr wouldn't kill her. He wouldn't kill Jill.

And he sure as hell wouldn't kill Billy.

Her arm burning as though it had been set aflame, Sarah swept her friend down the stairs and tried to ignore the footsteps rattling the house so close behind her.

Sarah had been able to outrun him pretty well before, and while going down the stairs, that still seemed to be the case—but there was no doubt about it. Jill weighed her down. As soon as Sarah set foot in the downstairs hall and had to readjust her grip of her friend, the truth became obvious to her in an instant.

She could try to haul her friend to the garage like she'd planned. The killer would either catch up on the way or pin her in the garage. Then, Sarah would be like a lamb in a slaughterhouse.

The alternative?

She could leave Jill.

Sarah's guilt was somewhat assuaged by her crass friend's groan. "Leave me *behind,* you fucking dip! Just—ugh—"

Sarah gasped as her friend let herself become nearly literal dead weight. Unwinding her arm from around Sarah's neck, Jill dropped backward across the landing of the staircase with a grimace.

"Just go," wheezed Jill, gripping her stomach. "It's fine, okay? I forgive you. I love you, even."

Sarah's eyes filled with sympathetic tears to see the ones rolling down her dying friend's face. "I love you, too, dude. Oh, man—"

Burr's foot appeared around the corner of the staircase.

Sarah booked it through the house without further sentiment, careening beyond the living room and out to the back yard.

As she burst through the kitchen's rear door and found herself once again alone beneath the night sky, Sarah realized she was practically on the verge of collapse. After pushing her muscles to their breaking point for so many minutes on end, Sarah was exhausted, winded, and extremely unsteady.

How long had it been? The night had felt like eternity. Now Sarah wondered if this, all the horror of Burr's invasion, had been unfolding for even half an hour.

Just standing was a tall order. She gave herself two seconds to brace against the door frame. Then, as she and Jill had at the start of all this, Sarah ducked around the fence line and followed it to the shed.

Man, those bolt cutters! Both girls had been dubious about their use as a weapon, but Sarah was grateful for them now. All the inanimate objects in the house, in fact! Oh, she appreciated them all so much. The house had seemed to be on her side all along.

Reassuring to know that somebody was.

After the cutters made quick work of the shed's padlock, she tossed them aside and smiled to let herself in.

In the semi-safety of the shed—if anything in her life could be considered even semi-safe again—Sarah flipped on the flashlight and swept its light across the contents of the cluttered room.

A handyman's workbench. An old-fashioned push mower. A coiled hose that served as the frame for a spider's web. A few paint cans too rusty to qualify for the basement.

A hatchet that gleamed in the light.

Sarah almost wept to yank it from the wall, not even considering the possibility of spiders that, a mere hour before, would have stayed her hand. While she set down the light to try the impromptu weapon's heft, however, that friendly flashlight illuminated something infinitely more valuable than even the red head of the axe.

"Bullets?"

Man, Sarah had lost it. She was officially talking to

herself—but oh, she didn't care!

Clutching the rattling box that was colored a red far more faded than the axe, than the killer's boiler suit, than the gas can that awaited her use, Sarah repeated in a happy, desperate whisper, "Bullets! Oh—"

Her fingers trembled. She pushed open the tiny cardboard casket within its case and gasped.

Six?

Six!

Six shots.

For a normal home invader, that would have been excessive. For Burr, it was a cruel joke. Sarah had upended an incredibly heavy liquor cabinet of wood and glass directly on top of him, yet the man didn't seem to have a scratch. Were six bullets really going to do the job?

The would have to.

Her hands shook as Sarah struggled to remember what Jill had done to check the cartridge. When she finally got it out she thought for a few harrowing seconds that she had broken it, but the babysitter swiftly realized where and how to load the bullets.

With trembling fingers, she pushed all six of them into the gun. She tried, anyway.

One dropped to the floor of the shed.

Swearing, Sarah whisked up her light and rooted around in the dust and dirt until she found it. As she loaded this final bullet into the clip, her terror-heightened senses detected the back door of the Johnson house opening from all the way across the lawn.

Sarah shut her eyes. Use some bullets now, or try the axe?

The answer was as obvious as it was frustrating... but the bullets were there to be used, and every second she delayed was another second closer to the one where she'd be cornered in this shed.

Every muscle in her body coiled like a set of springs, Sarah removed the belt from her pants. She looped it around her chest and shoulder with a trembling hand. Then, carefully, she slid the handle of the hatchet over her shoulder and made sure it could rest there without falling or hurting her.

With the axe crookedly hanging against her back in this makeshift sling, Sarah readied the gun and pushed open the door of the shack.

Upon finding Burr mere feet away, Sarah transmuted her wave of nausea into a squeeze of the trigger.

Sarah had never fired a gun before, but she'd watched other people do it in movies. Once she'd seen her uncle shoot some cans. That was years ago, though, when she'd been too small to try it herself.

The babysitter was totally unprepared for even that small pistol's kickback. Not only did she miss Burr completely but the gun bucked up in her hands until it almost hit her in the face.

Grimacing, Sarah stumbled back and tried to rectify her aim. She was too slow, too untrained.

And Burr was too relentless.

He closed the distance with another burst of uncanny speed. That kind of motion seemed impossible, given how slowly he lumbered around corners and up stairs...but Sarah had to reckon that it was a matter of momentum.

The very same momentum that made even Burr's rust-dulled knife sink so effortlessly into Sarah's left shoulder.

20.

FOR ONE second, two seconds, three, Sarah's brain struggled to fully grasp that she had been stabbed.

The burst of pain was so sudden and nightmarish that it was unreal. In fact, when she did realize that he'd gotten her, it seemed like a strange mistake.

This whole night, now that she thought of it, seemed like a strange mistake.

Arson, burglary, rape, murder: these crimes were horrors that happened to *other* people. Not to Sarah. Not to her friends. Being stabbed was simply not a physical possibility in the safe world of American suburbia where Sarah was raised.

But this was a new world.

This was a world that was infinitely more dangerous than the one she'd known before. It was a world that required her to be dangerous in response.

Her shoulder jerked forward while Burr yanked the knife out of the joint.

The killer drew his blade high to stab again.

Still somehow uncomprehending to both her injury and its gravity, completely numb with shock, Sarah pointed the gun. Her thumb slammed back the hammer.

Unhesitating, Sarah fired into the flesh of Burr's body without discrimination for her target. Lungs, stomach, heart, it didn't matter—she would take anything, anything at all.

She got his ribs.

Burr fell back a few steps as if in shock of his own. Gliding as effortlessly through the town as he had, perhaps he had forgotten that he had the capacity to receive injury as readily as he could deliver it.

Sarah longed to stick around and really prove that to him, but Burr was already starting to shake the pain off while her shoulder overflowed with ribbons of blood. The yellow and white shirt had been stained by Jill's mortal wounds, but now it absorbed the gouts from Sarah's fresh injury and communicated to her one crucial fact.

If Sarah was going to make it to the garage with the gas can—

Well. Then she was going to have to come back for it. Burr was closing in on her again.

Gritting her teeth, Sarah fired off a third round. She was satisfied that, while Burr hardly flinched, he did pause. It was a pause just long enough for her to tear back to the house, the wooden handle of the axe bobbing against her back every step of the way.

Sarah left the door hanging open. If she wasted even a second of her precious time to shut it, he'd just use the open window. By this point, she was about as keen on wasting time as she was on wasting blood.

Her shoulder burned with agony like she'd never felt. The previous slice of the knife was a joke now. Sarah felt as if pieces of the rust had lodged themselves in her shoulder joint, although that was surely the exaggeration of her imagination. Had to hope it was, anyway.

Struggling to avoid the sight of Jill's abandoned body lying unconscious or dead upon the floor, Sarah rushed up the stairs and found herself in the creepy bathroom again.

She had to admit that she was now sort of grateful for its bizarre lack of a mirror. If Sarah could have seen herself covered in blood, she never would have gotten the sight out of her head. No—she never would have been able to be so calm and matter-of-fact as she stripped off her makeshift holster along with her shirt while letting hot water surge from the tap.

Ears focused over the sounds, Sarah splashed the puncture and the prior slit in her arm with as much of the burning liquid as she could stand. Oh, it hurt! Hissing, she forced herself to do it again, again. As long as she could stand it: as long as she had time.

The hasty cleaning was anything but thorough, yet it would have to do. After washing away superficial blood flows and debris, Sarah double-checked the lock on the bathroom door and hurried through the motions of wrapping the wound. Good thing she'd taken a first aid class before starting to babysit!

Sarah maintained pressure on the puncture as best she could. The task was hard; her left hand was, while not completely out of commission, now significantly weakened and subject to bursts of pain every time it lifted too high. She fought through that pain to keep the injury covered with a messy wad of gauze. Meanwhile, with her other hand, Sarah wrapped the wound in a bandage. Blood began to soak through right away.

It would have to do. She had just replaced her shirt when a thump on the upstairs landing alerted her to Burr's presence.

The game had changed somehow. The fear was gone. It was all cold anger that she felt now: disgust and frustration. No more fear at all.

Sarah looked around herself. Then, considering the creepy casement window over the shower and the axe that she had set down to tend to her wounds, she snorted.

"Here's Johnny," Sarah muttered, hefting the axe as she faced the shower.

The bathroom doorknob rattled and the door itself soon shook under a great thump. Shoulder still burning, Sarah nonetheless stepped into the cramped, tiled stall, hefted the axe in both her hands, and brought its head to bear against the frosted glass of the casement window.

That was one sharp axe. Sarah was emboldened to see how immediately the pane broke, not shattering into a million pieces like movie glass but, all the same, spider-webbing on the first impact. A second strike knocked a few pieces out and a third had begun to ruin the frame just as the bathroom door produced a series of pained groans beneath Burr's incessant onslaught.

If the window hadn't been a casement and had just been a normal slider, Sarah might not have been able to fit through. Once she cleared the glass out, however, the opening proved to be at least the size of the laundry chute through which Sarah squeezed...and it was certainly friendlier, since there was no ominous tunnel involved.

You know...just a drop down from the second floor.

Couldn't be more than twenty feet, right?

You know—better to not estimate. Better to just do it.

Sarah boosted herself up while the bathroom door's hollow wood splintered beneath Burr's weight.

Vertigo swept her from head to stomach in a cold wave just to see the drop into the Johnsons' side yard. She didn't have any choice.

After tossing the axe, then the gun out of the window, Sarah considered the terrible height one more time.

This room was near the corner of the house. The garbage cans were almost right below her. If she could somehow throw herself out of the window and break her fall on those—

The bathroom door shattered.

Burr stepped inside.

Sarah had no more time to hesitate. She pushed herself up over the window frame, hissing as a piece of glass still stuck in the frame slit a fresh cut along her right side. Didn't matter, didn't matter. Just a cut. Keep going!

She reached up out of the window and grasped the house's siding, dragging herself out with a cry of victory that was too soon halted.

Burr's monstrous hand snatched the ankle of her jeans.

"No," screamed Sarah, her free leg thrashing wildly around.

It was incredible that, after all the fast moving he'd been doing, Burr still had so much strength. Sarah barely had any left. Certainly not enough to fend off the grown man trying to pull her back into the house.

She twisted in the window, screaming as that jagged shard cut another sharp line into her flesh. Now it opened a path around her waist and into her back, a fire that made her weep with agony.

From this new angle, Burr's grip managed to shift

from her jeans to her actual leg, but she got an advantage of her own. Her eyes linked with the horrific hollows of the clown mask. It smiled at her even though the animal glint behind bore not the least trace of humor.

Holding Burr's empty gaze, Sarah lifted her free foot and smashed the bottom of her shoe into that mocking mask.

The sole slammed so hard that she literally felt his nose snap beneath the pressure. Burr released his grip to touch his face through the mask. He quickly lifted it to feel the injury, but Sarah didn't stick around to see his face.

She didn't even turn around properly, which she regretted when she fell out of the window, dropped a story, and landed in the rose bushes lining the Johnsons' side yard. The thorny branches snapped beneath even her slight weight. Sarah groaned to see stars surely identical to the ones she had just shown Burr.

Every cell in her body ached. The roses had scratched up all the exposed flesh that Burr hadn't managed to wound. Her right ankle had twisted beneath her. Her teeth still seemed to rattle in her head.

But she'd made it out.

Yes—Sarah had made it out of the bathroom.

She was *outside.*

Heart throbbing with hope, Sarah leapt up beneath a final surge of adrenaline. Though stumbling and limping, she paid her injuries no further mind. Instead she groped around in the dark lawn.

Her hand touched the axe's wooden handle. Just to its left, she discovered the gun. With the latter stowed in the back of her jeans and the axe resting on her unwounded shoulder, Sarah dashed through the gate to the back yard.

It was loud, that gate. Its crash had been her first warning of Burr's presence. If the killer hadn't already been sure where she would try to go, Sarah was certain he now knew.

She didn't care. Nothing could stop her.

She'd get that gas can and get Billy out of here if it was literally the last thing she did.

There it was, still sitting red and pretty in the beam of the flashlight she'd abandoned with the abrupt arrival of the killer.

After tightening the impromptu holster of the axe to keep its bobbing handle still against her back, Sarah plucked up the gas can and left the flashlight behind.

By this point, she was used to the dark. By this point, she knew the Johnsons' house as well as she knew her own.

The only person who knew it better was its old owner.

Burr knew its every twist and turn. Its every creaking floorboard.

Sarah stepped through the house's still open back

door and removed the gun from the back of her jeans, her reflexes ready for any sign of movement. Her sneakers earned their title as she kept low, moving in total silence through the kitchen and living room.

Her mind was singularly focused on the garage.

On Billy.

On freedom.

Just as she glimpsed it all in the form of the garage door, Burr appeared from the hallway behind her.

The killer caught Sarah by the injured shoulder.

21.

PAIN PRODUCING the high scream that fear no longer could, Sarah raised the gun in her good hand. She fired on instinct.

The bullet whizzed through a wall.

Sarah's weapon was soon knocked uselessly from her hand. It slid across the hallway floor, splashed into the puddle of blood oozing around Jill's body, then lay still. The fire of Burr's powerful grip in the existing stab wound forced Sarah to also drop the gas can.

Though she sobbed with relief to see that the can had at least landed upright, that relief was short-lived. Twisting in Burr's grip, Sarah managed to catch, with both hands, the burly forearm raising the knife in preparation for a stab.

Sarah clenched her teeth at the exertion required to brace herself against the force of his arm. Even with both of hers pushing it away—even with the recent injury to his nose and the bullet wound that should have worked together to stagger him at least a little—Burr's strength was truly inhuman.

In fact, Sarah had to wonder if the adrenaline from the injuries she'd caused him hadn't just increased his strength. They certainly made him look more horrible.

Using both her good arm and her wounded arm to keep him at bay for as long as she could, Sarah stared into the face of the mask. Blood poured from Burr's broken nose and glistened down the happy mouth of the clown. The fluid had repainted its grimace with the same shining crimson that gave fresh life to Burr's red boiler suit. As if the mask, this terrible demon, had vomited the blood of the lives it had taken.

But it wasn't the mask, or a demon.

It was Burr—it was his injury.

Sarah released his arm to punch him in that injury as hard as she possibly could.

The incredible thing wasn't the risk Sarah took in releasing her grip of the killer's powerful arm to do this. It wasn't the feel of his blood, the additional crack of his bone beneath the mask, or the way he stumbled back.

It was the *noise* Burr made.

Just a short one. Barely a grunt. Yet, after all the screaming with which he'd filled the house—after all the suffering and horror and trauma he'd brought into Sarah's life—that grunt was more satisfying than anything she had ever experienced. She even smiled as she turned around to snatch up the gas can.

Fueling the car was going to be the issue, but maybe if she got the can started, supported it somehow, then locked herself into the car...

Well. First she had to get *to* the garage.

She was within four steps of it when a new burst of pain erupted in the back of her head.

The babysitter whipped around to discover with a cry that Burr had grabbed hold of her ponytail. With one hand, he dragged Sarah toward him. With the other hand, Burr lifted the knife to slit her throat.

Sarah's scream was so sharp that it almost concealed the sound of the gun's first discharge, but it didn't obscure the second.

Burr lurched forward, then back. His hand went limp around its grip of Sarah's hair. At last—at long last!—the killer's heavy body landed in the center of the hallway floor and seemed to shake the house upon its foundation while coming to rest.

Wide-eyed, Sarah whirled around as the gun tumbled from Jill's blood-soaked hand.

"Jill!" Gasping, Sarah rushed to the friend. Jill's head dropped back into the pool of blood before she made it over.

Her consciousness slipped in and out even as Sarah turned her upon her back. "Leave me."

It was the one phrase Jill said. Over and over.

Sarah tried, "Thank you," and Jill said, "Leave me."

"Thank you, oh, God, Jill—"

"Leave me!"

"Jill—" Sarah's tear-filled eyes lifted toward the garage.

Jill turned her limp head to the side, tried to shake it back the other way, then let it drop beneath its own weight. "Promise you'll leave me," she wheezed.

But—Sarah couldn't. She couldn't let her friend die alone. With Burr inert on the hallway floor, she remained kneeling there to hold her friend's hand.

"Okay," whispered Sarah. "Then I'll leave you. It's okay for you to die now, Jill. I'm going to be okay. I'll leave you behind. It'll all be okay."

In the corner of her eye, Burr's body twitched.

Sarah swore her tears reddened with anger.

Unaware of all this, Jill smiled and shut her faded eyes.

After touching her friend's wet cheek, Sarah rose unsteadily to her feet.

Sprawled in the hallway, bleeding from several bullet wounds in addition to his broken nose, Burr nonetheless reached for his knife. At the same time, Sarah removed the axe from its sling across her back.

She didn't even stop to think about it.

As she rushed up, the crimson blade of the hatchet raised above her head, the only thing Sarah thought about was Jill. Jill, now verifiably dead in the middle of the hallway.

Jill, her friend, an innocent teenager, dead forever: and Neoklaus Burr, somehow still alive.

Teeth bared, Sarah screamed in fury—a noise like a snarl as she brought the axe down to bear against the killer's back.

As with the gun, the ease of the motion was not the shock. It was the physical result of it. That was the horrific surprise.

When the axe's sharp red head hacked down into Burr's flesh, the impact rattled through Sarah's arms. She *felt* herself chopping into a man like firewood. An evil, sadistic, soulless man...but a man nonetheless. A human.

Yes: Sarah felt herself hacking up a human with an axe.

And she enjoyed it so much that she did it again.

Another, altogether different kind of force was required to yank the axe head out of Burr's back muscles, especially with a wounded arm holding her back. Sarah planted a foot on the murderer's neck to brace him down into the floor while she tore the weapon free of his body. The blade jerked free of the gaping wound with a wet vacuum *slurp.*

This time, when Sarah brought the hatchet down, the twitching body beneath her foot tremored. When this tremor passed, Burr lay still.

Teeth bared, Sarah popped the axe head out of Burr's meat and, after cleaving it down into his back muscles one last time, she left it there.

Coated almost head-to-toe in blood—hers, her friend's, the killer's—Sarah limped away from the body. She picked up the gas can on her way to the garage.

Sarah didn't pause. She didn't think about Jill. She had totally forgotten that Jack existed.

She hit the garage door button and, while it ground open, Sarah popped open the driver's side of the car to release the fuel door.

Billy sprang upright in from his hiding place in the back seat. While he boggled at the scarlet sight of her, he clung to the front seat, pressed himself to the window, followed her motions all around the car. All the time he begged to know, "Are you okay? Where's Jill? You're covered in blood! Is that a bandage? Where's the bogeyman?"

"Get back under the tarp, Billy," Sarah said calmly.

"But—"

"Don't argue with me."

Between her stern but somehow listless tone and her head-to-toe coating of blood, Billy seemed to decide it was, in fact, better not to argue with his babysitter. While he lay right back down and pulled the tarp over himself, Sarah tipped the can a bit higher.

Something thumped in the house.

Sarah didn't even care. She kept filling the tank.

By the time the can was empty, Burr had dragged himself to the garage door. With some struggle, he pulled himself upright against the frame. The hatchet remained lodged in his bleeding back. Between that and the clown mask, he looked like a man wearing a bizarre novelty costume.

Sarah removed the gas can from the vehicle and hurled it. The can spewed its odorous fluid across the garage and Burr's red figure. While he wavered back from it, she got into the driver's side of the car, took the keys from the driver's side visor, and twisted the ignition.

This time, the car started.

The engine roared to life along with Sarah's joy.

"Your dad sure is good at fixing stuff, Billy," she said idly, shifting the car into reverse amid the sudden clamor of the radio. She'd rolled out of the garage before Burr had even set foot into it.

"Uh-huh," agreed Billy softly.

Already muted by the tarp and his fear, Billy's answer was left almost inaudible beneath the blaring voice of the DJ. The radio host had been mid-announcement when the car turned on. Sarah grew aware of his words only after a few seconds.

"—but you don't want to listen to horror stories, or breaking news, or any of that jazz, baby…you tune into us here at KBBS to escape."

Despite herself, Sarah laughed. She looked over her good shoulder while she cruised back onto the street, then put the vehicle into forward gear.

"Let's lighten the mood with a couple of hits, shall we? Starting with this week's number one song on the Billboard charts, let's hear it for "Who Can It Be Now?" by Men at Work."

She twisted the volume up a little. At the end of the block, Sarah turned the car into the driveway of the house on the corner. "Do you like Men at Work, Billy?"

"Not really," said the boy, raising his voice over the funky music. "Can I sit up?"

"One more second."

In the distance, a towering figure stumbled down the Johnson's driveway and stood in its center.

Sarah pulled a neat three-point turn out of the driveway. She backed the car up a few more feet before putting it into forward gear.

"I don't super like them, either. But you know who I've been getting into the past couple of days? Fleetwood Mac. You should check them out."

She hit the gas and the car built speed immediately. By the time the headlights flooded his red figure, Neoklaus Burr had turned to run, axe still protruding from his back, across the grass of the lawn.

Sarah mounted the curb and soon thrilled at the speed-bump thump of his body falling beneath the bumper.

Somehow, she resisted the urge to back up and do it again. The temptation was very serious.

"Okay," said Sarah, twisting the steering wheel to roll back upon the street. "Now, you can sit up."

Sighing in relief, Billy shoved the tarp away while asking of the bump, "What was *that?*"

"Just some kind of pothole. Say...no chance you remember the number for Frank's Bistro, do you?"

"No," said the boy.

Sarah laughed, overjoyed to produce a noise that wasn't a scream, then glanced up in focused curiosity as something caught her eye. Flashing red and blue lights careened between the distant houses and stopped up on the corner.

"Well"—Sarah pulled over to flag down the long overdue cops—"then I guess they're going to be in for a real surprise when they get home."

22.

TURNED OUT that the cops weren't responding to Sarah's screams at all. As Lt. Breaker described it while she sat on the edge of the ambulance to receive on-site medical attention, "The old lady who lives at the house here called us in a fury...said a news van was parked in her oleanders, demanded we come make 'em move it."

Sarah stared him down, her eyes like daggers. "My friends died. Literally *died*. I was stabbed in the shoulder. I ran around that house screaming for I don't even know how long. I *threw myself out of a window*—and you didn't get *one single report?*"

Breaker spread his hands in a gesture that was as useless as it was infuriating. "People have the bad habit of assuming that somebody else is already calling the police in the case of an emergency like this.

They let other folks deal with it...now, who those 'other folks' are, I don't know."

It was amazing Sarah still had the capacity for anger. She was burned out from all the fighting and running, anxious about an imminent tetanus shot, and woozy from her blood loss—and frustration still overwhelmed her at the uselessness of anyone to help her.

While she stewed without offering a response, Breaker drew her out of her thoughts by touching her unwounded hand. "You did a very brave thing, Sarah. If you were my daughter, I'd be very proud."

About twelve yards away, blanket-wrapped Billy sat in the driver's seat of a police car as a special treat while an officer gingerly interviewed him about the night. Ignoring Breaker's well-meant praise, Sarah said, "I just hope this doesn't scar Billy for the rest of his life."

"It sounds to me like you did your best to keep him from being exposed to anything happening in the house tonight...and—well. You saved his life, Sarah." The girl still said nothing and Breaker continued, "I know it doesn't feel like much when your friends died tonight, but trust me when I say that it means everything. You're a hero."

"If I hadn't called my friends over, they'd still be alive."

Now it was Breaker's turn to be left speechless. What could he say? She was right.

With an empathetic frown, the cop patted her hand one more time, then glanced away. A police car had rolled up the street from the increasingly busy Johnson house. "It sounds to me like if you hadn't called your friends over, *you'd* be dead. Billy, too. Excuse me for a few minutes, Sarah, I'm sorry—"

While Breaker ducked away, another car careened around the corner and came to a sharp stop across the street. Billy perked in the middle of his conversation and threw the blanket away. Linda and Mark stepped from the familiar car.

"Mom! Dad!"

Sarah inhaled while Billy dashed into his father's arms. As the boy babbled to them, Sarah tightened her own blanket around herself and looked hopefully at the paramedic.

Upon the kind woman's nod, Sarah hurried after the boy.

"—and then Sarah made me hide in this little door—and did you *know* there was a little door under our stairs? Oh, oh, and—"

"Sarah," said Linda, the name a gasp as she crossed around the car.

At first, the elegant woman extended her arms to embrace the girl. She thought better of it when she noted, with a look of revulsion, the (mostly dried) blood that had inundated the teenager's outfit.

Instead, folding her hands over her heart, Linda stopped beside her husband and son. "Oh, Sarah! The police told us everything when they called us at the Bistro."

"We can't thank you enough," said Mark, his hand on the back of his son's head. "I can't believe you had to go through all of that. You were very brave."

Brave! Mark was the second person to call her that so far.

Sarah already hated it. She didn't like the thought of being a hero. She had stuck an axe in a man's back and felt the impact rattle along the muscles of her weakened arms. She had enjoyed it, a fact that she had already decided to never relate to anyone. No: no matter the context that had engendered the feeling.

The last thing Sarah wanted was to be applauded. Maybe this was why Jill's father had become a long-haired hippie after coming back from Vietnam.

And even worse than applauding her act of violence was what the Johnsons had said without realizing.

'The police told us *everything*.'

'I can't believe you had to go through *all of that*.'

As if they could know what 'everything,' 'all of that,' even was! As if anyone could ever understand.

If the Johnsons hadn't gone on a date that night, all three of them would have died.

While the family embraced before her eyes, Sarah knew that fact with absolute certainty.

"So," began Sarah. Mark and Linda both smiled up at her, parental gratitude shining from their faces. She stared them hard in the eyes one at a time and, settling on Mark, said, "About my payment."

"Oh! Oh. Aha. Of course!" With a slight cough and a glance askance, Mark passed the clinging boy to his wife and removed his wallet from his trousers. "It was, uh—how much again?"

Sarah wondered how much blood still coated her face. Mysteriously, Mark remembered without her having to answer him.

"Oh, yes, that's right...I remember now—here—"

As Mark thumbed through the thick collection of bills in his wallet, Sarah reminded him, "And last time, too."

"Of course," said Linda in a forced tone of chipper agreement. "Yes, of course! So sorry we forgot."

"I just can't believe we're so air-headed," agreed Mark, doubling the fee for the night. "And you know—you know, let me throw in a little extra. We owe you so much, after all."

Sarah inhaled with relief while he stacked the bills in her hand. They seemed to weigh about as much as a motorcycle. She counted them right then and there to be sure.

Satisfied, she put the money away.

"Thanks, guys," she said, glancing toward the cluster of cops at the corner. Most of them watched her, waiting for her to finish the conversation.

Especially the lieutenant.

Breaker cupped his hands around his mouth to

call, "Sarah!"

"I should go."

While she turned away, Billy called, "Wait—"

The boy tore out of his parents' clutches and dashed to hug her around the waist.

Sarah grimaced. He gripped her bandaged cut from the glass of the bathroom window, but it didn't matter. Nothing mattered. The kid was alive.

She knelt in the street to return Billy's embrace, holding him to her good shoulder and inhaling against the tears of joy that threatened her carefully maintained countenance.

They had made it.

"Thank you, Sarah," whispered Billy. "I love you. You're the coolest, best babysitter ever. I'm sorry I called you a scaredy-cat."

"Oh! It's okay, little dude. Love you, too."

With a ruffle of his hair, she stood. Sarah's first genuine smile in what felt like an eternity was produced for Billy. "I'll see you around, okay?"

Nodding rapidly, the boy dashed back to his waiting parents. Sarah waved at them before returning to Breaker's side of the street.

The lieutenant's voice was low as he guided Sarah toward his cruiser to talk in semi-private. "Well...I'm afraid I have some bad news, but it won't come as a surprise. We've confirmed your friends' deaths. I'm very sorry."

Sarah nodded. Jack had been obvious, but Jill—Jill

had clung on to life so long, so tenaciously! Sarah had nursed a sliver of hope for Jill's possible survival.

Realistically, Sarah had accepted it was an impossibility from the first moment she set eyes on her friend's prone body across the Johnsons' bedspread... but the human spirit is nothing if not prone to futile dreams.

Even if Sarah still had the strength left that night to feel sorrow, Breaker's next words would have interrupted any such internal rumination. "Now—where did you say Burr's body was, again?"

The visceral reaction this question produced within Sarah's body was one related not just to her stomach but to all her internal organs. Her liver, her kidneys, her lungs and heart: they all seized up along with that often-cited sack of bile.

Sarah glanced reflexively up the street, then back at Breaker's face. "Right there. Right there in the middle of the yard! You can't miss him."

"Well...apparently, we did."

"What? What do you mean?"

"I mean, by the time back-up responded to the crime scene at the Johnsons' house, Burr's body was gone. My guys are searching the property right now... it's possible that he dragged himself somewhere to hide, but—"

The words bursting from her in a rage, Sarah demanded, "After *I* shot him, after *my friend* shot him, after I hit him with an axe *and* with a car—he's still out there? He just—just got up and *walked away?*"

"Well, after all the hell you gave him, I'd be pretty surprised if he just got up and walked. But..."

While the lieutenant trailed off unhelpfully, Sarah wondered if anger like this was the cause of the phenomenon known as spontaneous human combustion. Was it possible to burst into flames of pure anger?

Sarah wondered numbly about that—but she didn't have to wonder about Burr.

Breaker may have thought it impossible for Burr to get up and walk into the night like any other man, but Breaker hadn't been through all the things Sarah had been through that night.

He hadn't seen what Burr was capable of. He hadn't seen, experienced, *felt* what it was like to be in the house with that horrific masked killer. Breaker hadn't had to see Burr dragging himself to his feet while Jill died in a pool of her own blood.

"What are you going to do?" Sarah waved her hand off into the darkness and struggled to keep her voice low with respect to the Johnsons. The couple talked nearby to a pair of officers, presumably about hotel arrangements while their house remained an active crime scene. An eavesdropper until the end, Billy glanced toward her at the sharp pitch of her voice.

Trying to contain herself, eyes glowing with the fury that seeped from her every pore, the blood-soaked babysitter continued in a hiss, "You can't just let him run free out there! Look at what he's done—to

Jill, to Jack! Look at this town! You guys have to *stop him!* What are you waiting for?"

"Now," said Breaker, the compassion of his tone crossing the line from comforting to condescending, "how about you just let us worry about that, Sarah…I know you've had a long night."

Turning away, Breaker waved a hand toward the paramedics who gossiped against the back of their ambulance.

While they arrived to help Sarah into the back of the emergency vehicle, the lieutenant assured her warmly, "For now, why don't we go ahead and take you to the hospital? Get your injuries looked at a little more closely…you'll be safe there."

As the paramedics guided her into the ambulance, Sarah wasn't sure she'd be safe anywhere.

Not anymore.

PUPPET COMBO®

Influenced by slasher movies and low-poly survival horror titles from the PS1 and PS2 eras of gaming, Puppet Combo® is a prolific studio whose titles range from such nightmarish offerings like POWER DRILL MASSACRE to the more conceptually surreal FEED ME, BILLY. BABYSITTER BLOODBATH is the company's first collaborative novelization. Check out Puppet Combo®'s website for more on its games, including BABYSITTER BLOODBATH—then, support the creation of new games (and get tons of fantastic content) by contributing to their Patreon!

REGINA WATTS

Regina Watts is an author of transgressive and splatterpunk fiction, and a longtime fan of Puppet Combo®'s games. If you enjoyed this novelization, be sure to explore Regina's work on Amazon—especially her depraved DOTTIE FOR YOU, a serialized horrotica perfect for fans of splatterpunk. Get free stories by signing up for her newsletter, and don't be shy about leaving a nice Amazon review if you enjoyed BABYSITTER BLOODBATH: it's an easy way to help both creators at the same time!

Made in the USA
Columbia, SC
25 April 2022

59359940R00129